SCREAMING EAGLES WINGS

DAVID ROSE

Publisher: Dead Reckoning Collective
Book Cover Artwork & Design: Tyler James Carroll
Editor: Michael Ramos

Printed in the United States of America

Library of Congress Control Number:
2024948475

ISBN-13: 978-1-963803-07-5 (paperback)

PRAISE FOR SCREAMING EAGLES WINGS

"For a work of fiction, this book not only takes the reader to what the battle of Fallujah was actually like, but it also deals with what many of us Fallujah vets dealt with years later after the battle."

-SSG James Amyett,
1st Infantry Division, 3rd Brigade Reconnaissance Troop (ret)

"Screaming Eagles Wings stands out as one of the most compelling and thought-provoking novels on the Iraq War, bringing readers face-to-face with the harsh realities of urban combat and how it fundamentally changes those who survive."

-Alex Saxby,
Author of *Fallujah Memoirs,* career Infantry Officer, and veteran of Operation Phantom Fury

AUTHOR'S NOTE

This book is a work of fiction.

And this book has a lot to do with Fallujah's retaking, and the days leading up to it, and the days and years after. And to tell such a tale one must tell also of the GWOT, of Iraq, of the minds of men who fought there, and other things which we love to prattle on about. There is no single book, however, fiction or otherwise, that can tell the whole tale of the Global War on Terror, or of Iraq, or of the Second Battle of Fallujah; known to many as Operation Phantom Fury. But this trim novel aims its sights at that city, as its author once did, as many who hold this book once did too.

Of Bags and Grass, Murray and delightful Jim, none exist. Nor does Gunny, though their counterparts do; the men for whom this book was ultimately written. Those men, the last generation to play in parks before such places were rounded of their hard edges, the generation called to action by *Fight Club* as much as 9/11; a ragtag few who, I hope, will understand why the warriors who await are so cheerful overseas.

Pardon me for the high dollar word, but veteran or not, like it or not, we are all floating now in a "postmodern" sea, clinging to the debris of our former traditions. This is why I chose to embed flashbacks and forwards in the places where I did, to illustrate all the clearer that in such nihilism (having proved the mighty left-hand of Progress), sacrifice and honor, adventure herself, shined that much brighter as the highpoint in many of our young lives. Those same men, not so young now…well, they have Bags and his loyal team to take them back into that city once more.

This book is about the Marine Corps and about Marine Recon, but at the same time it isn't. With regards to the recon community, much better accounts can be found in a high number of other works. I merely put Bags and his team into such muddy boots because for this story to work the teams needed to be small, to operate virtually alone, and that I simply was never in the grunts (the noble bulk of who actually fought in Fallujah), which made my decision easy.

I am not the ultimate veteran of Phantom Fury. Far from it. I didn't storm the city, nor did I stalk its streets like, say, the soldiers of 1st Infantry Division or the grunts of 1st Battalion 8th Marines. I was more like Murray on Benchmark 42—which was a real place, and possibly still is.

With the 20-year anniversary of Phantom Fury upon us, though, I felt something was in order. A celebration perhaps, or perhaps not.

Spent Shell Casings—retitled *No Joy* by its second publisher —is a source I pulled from at times. A recon battalion did in fact deploy to Iraq in late 2004. And though the events that follow are not historically accurate, in their own way I believe them to be true. True in the mood they invoke. True to the era in which they paint—one liar's brush stroke at a time, until the larger truth is there. The lessons learned. How to cast our eyes and look forward: the way fairy tales once taught us the oft-brutal vagaries of real life. For this book, more than anything, is a fairy tale.

—David Rose, March 2024

SCREAMING EAGLES WINGS

or

IN AND OUT OF FALLUJAH

Tyler Boggs corrals his kids, and out of his home office they go. It's the weekend, plus it's early afternoon, which means they've been nothing but energy for hours. After they've scampered away he shuts himself in. He calls from the other side of the door, telling his wife it's going to be a while.

Fall in Florida is still everywhere else's summer. With the heat index, the air outside is nipping at close to ninety degrees. He looks out the window for a time, seeing the bright sun shine off every car and boat and mailbox owned by his neighbors. He turns toward his desk and then he stares at *the* wall; all the pictures, plaques, awards, and a tacked-up AL FALLU-JAH map that has come loose at one end and is flapping in the AC. Al Fallujah—or just Fallujah. It has been twenty years, almost to the minute, since Tyler and his team had set foot in that city.

He walks over and opens his closet. There is a stack of books from his days at the Amphibious Reconnaissance School up in Fort Story, Virginia; back when he was a student and becoming a Recon Marine. The school is gone now, absorbed into another over on the West Coast. But his old books are still with him; instruction manuals on patrolling, communication, land navigation, and amphibious such and such that reminds him of a shark that rubbed against him while off the coast of Onslow when Battalion was neck-deep in summer training. Next to the books are cammies folded on the floor; the digital green and desert uniforms he'd worn right before getting out; both still with their gold jump wings and gold dive bubble pinned on the chest. Ordained on a hanger is a lone blouse, one without badges. The bullet hole in its unwashed fabric stares at him like an inquisitor leaning forward an eye; unflinching, saying, "I, too, remember." One who remembers how baby-faced boys shed fat in boot camp to learn for a while that they could run like the wind, remembers a man picking up another's rifle as fast as a bullet could tear through a desert-digi blouse, Humvees pegged out on long dark roads, mortars that flew, the young, coffin-nail warriors whose exhilaration flew higher than the mortars themselves.

Among the clutter is a small Tupperware box. He picks up the box and cracks open the lid. Inside are three Purple Hearts, two gas caps—one shot off an old motorcycle—and there's an old PSYOPS leaflet in there, too.

Tyler Boggs, or "Bags" as his teammates had once called him, had been a Recon Marine. As a team leader in a recon battalion, Tyler had seen more of Phantom Fury than most. The Retaking of Fallujah, as it was known, had been the bloodiest fight for the Marine Corps since Vietnam. With the exception of a few grunt units and a ragtag cohort of attachments, Tyler and his teammates had been uniquely baptized in a deeper shade of red.

Now, two decades later: smartphones and social media apps and new frontiers to war over. And birthed too were many children, soon taking from Tyler and his ilk the role of those who were the young women and men. Fallujah seemed like it was looming just over the horizon, though, all that while, as it seemed loomed the men, those whom he'd served with on perhaps his greatest adventure. Their faces were always near, smiling, bright-eyed, but the time had come to remember them marred by dust and blood.

There were so many faces, so many names he once yelled out with a whole heart. And he remembers them all. But only those closest appear now, for his mind is gathering, gathering up the smoke and the sand and the gunpowder of past days, squeezing them into something like a diamond, with heartbreaker hands, focusing his memory.

He turns back to his desk. On it is a stack of pages, typed on for the past six months. Now it is done. He sits down, ready to read. He nestles in his chair, and as he does he reflects on when he was known endearingly only as "Bags" as does a diamond caught upon the rays of the sun. Many angles. Many flashes. In one bright flash he's hurling himself out of a plane before the war, sliming along its side like a bug on a windshield until suddenly parachuting to the earth. Then another flash, then another. Another flash, a different memory, now hot and white, front and center; one of war and the thereafter. He's thinking about a funeral, death itself, about how not all who fought made it home.

Summer in North Carolina was hot, especially on the coast. The type of heat where it always felt like it was about to rain but never did. The grass in the landing zones was long and green and the trees in the training areas were tall, and the tank trails cut through them straight and white, as if the Camp Lejeune engineers of old had made them as a love letter to track-wheeled power. Camp Lejeune hugged the Atlantic, and no closer could one get to the ocean than the recon barracks of Courthouse Bay. A hot green summer; mid-August in fact, in the Year of Our Lord 2004. The clock on the wall read 1900, though not a single Marine in the rec room was looking at anything other than Grass's hideous, infected nut.

The whole team gathered around. Doug Murray was there. Bags was there, too. So was Ted James, holding Ian Pendergrass's scrotum in one hand, a sharp knife in the other.

It had been a quiet Sunday evening, quiet as barracks went. Monday morning's looming formation subdued those who were still milling about, scratching their freshest haircuts. *Had been quiet*, but Pendergrass, or "Grass" as everyone from the newest admin clerk to the battalion sergeant major called him, had hopped on his Cannondale and ridden too long, too hard, while slightly drunk, and had worn instead of Aquaphor and liner shorts only denim jeans and his own sweat. The result was a monstrous abscess on his testicle, and him howling in agony. The Battalion Aid Station wouldn't be open for another twelve hours and a trip to Main Side to wait in the hospital would have felt like a stretch toward eternity. So someone proposed a hip-pocket class. If it wasn't for Murray's blond hair and Grass's brown, the two could have passed for twins. Both were tall, brawny, and both looked down with morbid curiosity at James as he steadied his hand and brought his head lower.

"Jim," Grass broke in, "you sure you know what you're doing?"

"I believe so." James went by Jim the same way Grass went by Grass. Short for a Recon Marine, the stocky, round-faced now-surgeon was known battalion-wide for his good nature. His ability to safely cut through tissue, though, was yet to be tested. "A corpsman over at Force showed me, said he had to do it once while on ship." Jim wiped his face and bit his bottom lip.

"Oh," Murray said, wincing. "Oh, man." Murray was still holding his M4, not the one Battalion had issued, but his personal. He'd been doing mag changes while sitting on a couch with his sights kept on a dot on the wall. He now hugged that rifle, leaning into Bags as they both laughed and almost puked.

"There we have her," delighted Jim, slicing open Grass's sac and letting ooze forth a white putrescence. "Bags," Jim said with the animation of a doctor working a patient, "the stuff, if you please."

Even though Bags was the team leader, he and his guys operated in a way that baffled most others. Normally six men, teams had been rearranged into four and five to fit into the Humvees that were waiting for them over in Iraq. A team of four men, Bags figured, was that much better. So Bags was TL, Jim assistant TL, Murray was the radio operator, and Grass was considered point man when not churning out infected testicles under his denim shorts, and none of those titles made much difference to any of them. They were four equals, for as many occasions as the world would allow. Bags handed Jim a shoebox full of medical supplies.

Before long, Grass was "cured" and someone handed him a beer. They all laughed and plopped down on the couches, and no sooner had their asses hit the cushions than the doors to their rec room swung open.

It was Hendershot, a clown from their platoon. By the looks of him, he was still on duty over at battalion head-quarters; a place that was beyond the parking lot and down a tank trail a good quarter mile away. Less than a week ago he'd wrecked his car going almost a hundred down HWY 17, out by Holly Ridge. He was lucky to be alive, let alone be able to run his driver's-license revoked ass all the way to the barracks. But nonetheless, there he stood, in his green cammies, panting, trying to catch his breath.

Finally, he straightened himself and blew out, "We— Fallujah's gonna be retaken!"

Bags didn't know at the time the full picture. Few did. Years later, when the dust and carnage had settled, Bags would know that on 28 April 2004, the first battle of Fallujah had ended and an agreement had been made with the Fallujah Brigade to keep insurgents out of the city. That brigade had been stood up by local Iraqis and the net they set had holes in it a mile wide. At the time, Bags knew Battalion was heading over to Iraq. He and his guys knew the area they were going to work in would put Fallujah next to their shoulders, but Hendershot's words were someone saying Fallujah wasn't going to be in the background but smack-dab center.

"Shut the hell up," they all said.

But the team was on their feet, asking Hendershot to slow down. He stopped gasping and soon told them his tale. He was indeed on duty over at headquarters, and there had just been an emergency meeting. He was supposed to walk the halls and man the duty desk, but all the higher-ups showing up in civilian clothes sent him tiptoeing to put his ear against a locked door.

"They all talked for hours," he said. "We sure-as-shit are going into Fallujah."

"Are they still there?" Bags asked.

"No. Just left. Why I ran over."

Grass pulled out his cell phone and wiggled it. "You know, you could have called."

"My phone got lost in the wreck."

They all laughed, including Hendershot, who now breathed normally.

Amidst the high spirits, though, Bags was thinking. Weird perhaps, but high school had gone on so slow. The Division's change of command ceremony a month or so ago had slogged on so miserably he almost broke from his position to check if he still had a pulse. These were strange things to think about, and he pulled himself back out of his head.

Hendershot had noticed Murray's M4 and all talk shifted to killing and being killed, about who had trained the hardest and who'd shot the truest and they talked about how they hoped their work would be seen. Bags agreed with his guys, all they were saying, to a man, but he was unsure if they would understand what path his own mind was trekking. Through school, through ceremonies, through it all, it was as if one molasses-dripping yoke lifted to be replaced by yet another. But war? Could war be where the dullness of modern life itself went to die?

Bags sat back down. He could feel the tightness of his running shoes. He listened to someone's engine, revving out in the parking lot—as if they too had heard Hendershot's news. It may all happen. He didn't want to kill anyone, not really. That was just a maybe. Something that might come with the uniform. What he wanted was to find that place where intensity and mastery met and then became one. Even recon, though so very close at times, had yet to birth this gift. It was perhaps war where it would come. He wanted war; adept, capable, able, with brothers at his side, to move and report and shoot if needed. To *move*. To move through Iraq like lightning.

By Tuesday, training had intensified, and Battalion locked in an extra week of MOUT.

Military Operations on Urbanized Terrain: Bags and his team, along with platoon after platoon, walked through a town of particle board until they'd shot hundreds of blanks and had fully memorized each and every window. Exercises varied. MOUT town consisted of a main road and a few muddy offshoots. Hugging both sides of every path were the cheap wooden buildings, some two-story but most buildings one; all riddled with doorways and parapets. Sometimes the Marines patrolled the dirt roads on foot. Others, Higher would have them roll through in vehicle convoys, usually with the first or last Humvee taking fire. Whatever group wasn't playing Enemy assumed the role they all knew awaited them: patrollers and door-kickers, and the rumors that had spread landed on flat dead truth one day when the colonel himself held a formation. Their battalion would participate in the retaking of Fallujah.

Rooftops were aimed at more. Rifles were pointed and blanks were fired at everyone who moved in the mud and wood of that training town, and with a renewed fervor. A weeklong combat medical course was squeezed in after only two punitive days. Wills were made. BBQs were canceled, replaced by long runs down tank trails; rifles in hand, and running shoes replaced by tied-tight boots. Men drank and cheered and bench pressed and feared, and then on September 11, 2004, like a shot they were "over there."

They'd taken civilian planes at first. From North Carolina to Germany to Kuwait, where they felt their first blast of desert wind. In Kuwait, every damn thing was earned. The platoon who shot the highest got the best GP tent. The team within that platoon who had the most senior team leader took the cots nearest the fan. The most ardent brawler under that team leader took the comfortable cot of his choosing. In a sand-licked whirlwind, Bags saw it unfolding before his very eyes: he imagined all the people back home, sulking over how awful it was that those brave boys had to suffer overseas. Those same boys laughed and smiled, did pushups inside GP tents until their knuckles bled, cleaned the desert sand from their weapons until their metal shined again cool and black.

Soon they were up in the air once more, this time in C-130s. Those gray monsters took them over the very places they would soon patrol, then did a series of combat maneuvers until the planes had spiraled down to a guarded airfield and soon after their boots touched the sand of Iraq.

It was night when the trucks came: one of those fall desert nights where the moon is faded so that stars shine in a black overrun. There they loaded and soon crawled out the gates.

The convoy was large, too large for one to see its beginning or its end, for Bags tried through his night vision goggles, but twists and turns in the road hid much from view. And then finally they were at the gates of Camp Fallujah, a massive compound a few miles away from the city that gave it its name. It was a land of barriers and gravel, grays and browns put in contrast by the bright white trailers that formed seemingly endless rows. Even in the night air, this world of white shapes lay plain to the naked eye. It would be their home, where they'd hang hat and head when not stalking the farmlands outside the wire. A cluster of about twenty trailers was set aside for their battalion, each trailer having been sundered by two aluminum walls; allowing three rooms per.

As the moon set, the colonel, Battalion's head man, pulled out a sheet of paper and made good his promise. Eyeing the list, he read off the team at the very top.

Because Murray had practiced with his rifle more, because they *all* had practiced with their weapons more; shining upon the ranges, because they hungered to learn, be it field expedient antennae or how to perform rec room medical operations, because they ran longer and harder than even their recon peers, and because Bags asked them to keep their uniforms forever clean, Battalion let Bags's team choose the first trailer. The battalion moved in after.

The battalion moved in, and much happened. When the sun rose, Bags wondered if he were looking up at the same burning sun he'd seen when they'd all left North Carolina. It was strange to be in a land so foreign yet where things were so familiar. In fact, much was: the smell of Humvee exhaust as they growled on by, the chatter of Marines from different units, walking in groups to or from the bustling chow hall. He'd known they weren't heading to Vietnam. There, at least, would have been green jungles and many squawking birds. Iraq, or inside Camp Fallujah anyway, appeared a rather bleak place. Gravel grey and HESCO barrier brown. Trailer park white.

But none could deny the effort that different militaries had thrown on it, trying with some success to beautify a colossal square of utility and potential death. There were hedges. There were rows of trees lining main thoroughfares; the roads with double yellow lines in the middle like they were still in a world where drivers cared. Schools of small birds, reminding Bags of swallows, flew about the place; grabbing sticks with their beaks to nest somewhere in the trailers.

There was no shortage of buildings either. Most were long and low, with many rooms on both sides of a central hallway. These quickly became the battalion offices. Anywhere from the operations room to the chaplain, the armory to the office where Bags and the rest of their platoon would meet prior to every mission. It was a world of white walls and mopped tile floors and AC units rattling day and night.

When not inside one of these, the Marines busied themselves outfitting their pods; Jim and Bags in one, Murray and Grass in the one next door. Separated by that slim metal wall; they hooted and hollered from both sides, demanding the others come over to merrily discuss future operations or gather round and watch a movie on Jim's portable DVD player.

There were many meetings; company meetings, platoon meetings, right on down to team meetings, then they all were gathered in one last battalion cluster where they all stood in a large circle around the colonel and thus learned on the morrow they'd be stepping outside the wire and officially entering the war.

On the eve of their last night, their last night before beginning the very first of their many missions, Gunny Ulfe had everyone meet in the platoon office.

Gunny Ulfe was their platoon sergeant. Bags's team was one of four in the platoon, and of those four Ulfe was unquestionably in charge. Sure, there was their lieutenant, called just "LT" by everyone. LT was a good man, but all knew Gunny Ulfe was both mother and father.

"As you all know," Ulfe said, spitting out his dip. Everyone in the platoon was pushed to one side of the already cramped room; sitting on the floor or on stacks of water bottles. Everyone except for Gunny, who stood at the other end in front of a vast map. With the time he'd racked up as a drill instructor, and that he had the square-jaw face of a bulldog, it amused Bags without relent that their platoon sergeant was a Marine Corps mascot if ever had there been one. "As you all know," the mascot said, "tomorrow morning we begin our seven months of operations. The main focus will eventually be Fallujah, but much will come before it. Our platoon has been tasked with weapons caches."

Grumbles, whispers, furtive talk all filled the room. They'd been briefed on enemy caches by everyone from Gunny to LT to Marines who upon their arrival were beginning their own trek home. It had been a source of confusion: what were they supposed to actually call the enemy? To Bags and his team, it made little sense calling someone "terrorist" if they were armed with an AK-47 and were willing to fight you head-on. Due to the support of British troops and various others, the war effort had been coined "coalition forces." It was a mouthful, "anti-coalition forces;" a term favored by LT and most of the other officers. But nobody actually called them that; the men who awaited the Marines with roadside bombs and rifles ready. "Mujahideen" was the popular one, shorted simply to Muj. It was the Muj they were after. It was the Muj who were currently fortifying the dreaded Fallujah. And it was the Muj, they were now told, who stockpiled metric tons of weapons and ammunition out in the farmlands.

"The Muj," Gunny Ulfe was saying, "and their sympathizers, they are digging into the berms, loading them up, covering it back up then high-tailing it before any of us can get there. This has been ongoing, but word has come down they're intensifying said efforts. They are making stockpiles for their buddies in Fallujah, and it's a worry said stockpiles will seep into the city just prior the war."

The *war* had been going on for over a year now, but all knew Ulfe meant the mayhem that was coming. The noose had already begun to tighten. Gunny Ulfe was no longer speaking. He stood in front of his Marines and waited for questions.

"Gunny," Bags rose to his feet and thus spoke. "Are we getting any engineers? I can't imagine just walking around the berms, hoping to find everything."

"We are getting engineer attachments and more," Gunny said. "Each engineer will have their combat-grade metal detector and a shovel too. Anything y'all find will get blown up by the EOD boys that'll either be with us or one radio transmission away from me and LT here."

Grass leaned toward Murray. "What's EO—"

"Explosive Ordnance Disposal," Murray whispered back.

Grass nodded and Bags sat down, both fixing their eyes squarely on Gunny when he said, "We will likely encounter the Alzilal."

"…The what?" Someone asked.

"The who?" asked someone else, masking a giggle.

"You may not find them so funny," Gunny said. "They're a specific Muj group, one who don't talk on phones—which will make them harder to track. Word is they're good at mortars."

This caused a stir. It was a strange thing, spending countless hours on the ranges and in shoot houses; dialing in one's accuracy to the point of being a rifle master. Yet it wasn't gun battles that most likely awaited the Marines. Instead of Wild West-like shootouts, there were all sorts of nasty replacements. One was improvised explosive devices, which would become known infamously as IEDs, ranging from bombs that could tear the turret off a tank to hodge-podge wires sticking out the rear end of a donkey. The other replacement was getting mortared. This struck certain Marines with a particular kind of fear. Once an enemy mortar was launched out from a mortar tube, the only thing standing between a miss and a grizzly fate was cold hard math: the angle of the tube, the distance between the launcher and their target. The thought of just standing there when flying metal came raining down was bad enough, that a dedicated group was known for this sinister tool was far worse.

Gunny continued, "The Alzilal shoot out a barrage then pack up and dilute back into the farmlands like shadows. They do this so fast, that as of yet, no one's been able to catch 'em." He nodded directly at Bags when he said, "We hope to change that. This is why when your engineers are on the hunt you'll be on the lookout for those bastards."

When the meeting was over the Marines dispersed. Some went to the camp gym while others returned to their rooms. "I wonder if we'll see any of those...Azzies, or whatever?" Jim said. He held the door open as Bags shuffled in. Then he shut the door and locked it. "We got a plan for them, Bags?"

Bags didn't answer. He was looking at his flak jacket and his helmet, wondering if they were enough armor to fend off an accurate mortar blast. Bags and Jim could hear Murray and Grass carrying on in the next room over, carrying on like they'd just learned of a merry outing.

"Those two are nuts," Bags laughed, unbuttoning his blouse.

And after a fitful night's rest, the alarm clock went off and the team along with Gunny Ulfe and the rest of their platoon were rolling out of camp. They'd been assigned Humvees at dawn and were breaking them in. The air was hot; a dry heat that didn't pummel them as they'd half-expected. The sun had long since risen over the brown land, and now it watched on. Bags's Humvee was an uparmor; a warhorse in comparison to the bare open-backs some of the others had been given. Though sealed in its metal with windows still up, a wind came in from the open turret and wrapped around them the morning air.

Like all team leaders, Bags was up in the front passenger seat. He'd done his best to memorize maps but now that they were rolling down the hardball to god knows where the whole thing looked altogether weird. Sure, there were those power lines, and yes they kind of paralleled the road they were on, and yes, too, it appeared this road was a main artery, for now, but there were many things the maps didn't tell.

Dirt roads, which closer resembled trails, shot off from the hard ball which led to settlements so small they could hardly be called a village. What was more, new roads—paved ones—and a host of new settlements had sprouted from the ground like mushrooms. He eyed a water tower on the map and then called up to the turret, "Grass, two o'clock. See a water tower?"

Grass, seen by all in the Humvee as only rump and legs, soon yelled down, "Yup, more three o'clock, though. It's a bit out."

"Good enough," Bags said.

Jim looked over from the driver's seat. "Making sure we ain't lost?"

"Making sure I have the right map. This whole area's a mess."

Along with the team was their combat engineer. If it weren't for the fact that he looked like he was fifteen he would have been a right recruiting poster, something said almost verbatim by Jim when they'd welcomed him aboard. He was like all the engineers they'd seen that morning; high and tight hair, walking inside a green flak vest, and strapped with an old M16 and an olive-drab metal detector. The engineer had already been in country a month, but he'd told them this was his first trip outside the wire, and after he only sat quietly and looked out his window.

Murray, sitting behind Bags and manning the radio, unglued his ear from the handset. "Sounds like it's gonna get a whole lot messier. I think Gunny's lost."

Bags hadn't even noticed they'd come to a halt: five Humvees, puttering in idle.

"What you think he's doing?" said Jim.

The order would change, but for Day One the lead vehicle was LT, the platoon corpsman, the platoon communications bubba, and Gunny Ulfe; all crammed together. Other platoons split their leadership into two Humvees, but Gunny and LT had said from the go that keeping the teams together was a priority, and now the team in front of Bags's and the two teams behind them all waited. Murray could be seen in the rear-view mirror, looking about with the radio handset still pressed to his ear as he looked at every clump of dirt or bag of trash.

Bags called up at Grass, hoping from that height he could explain what was going on up ahead. But it was Murray who answered. "Okay, moving. They weren't sure if the dirt road we're taking was the right one or not."

"Suppose it is," Jim said, soon turning the wheel and following the vehicle in front of them. It was a bumpy yet uneventful ride, with the only high note of passing an old tractor.

Predeployment classes had informed them how IEDs would be lying in wait, stuffed in the guts of parked vehicles. Grass had most certainly remembered, sliding down inside their Humvee, until the coast was clear and they were all laughing as he get back up there to "be a man." The movement came to an end. The convoy formed a wide circle on a low mound, wide enough so one Humvee-killing mortar wouldn't take out the rest. There, they put their Humvees in park and the Marines prepared for their first patrol.

Bags had asked Jim to check the team. Bags had even

given them a second check before they'd all left after breakfast. It felt silly in a sense; they'd done so much training back in the US that inspections had become more a reflex than an obligation. Bags knew Grass's SAW would be hanging on its sling and two spare drums would be on his flak. Murray would have the team radio; handset clipped near enough his ear so that he could hear anything directed to the team. All their M4 rifles would be black and clean; their optics full of fresh batteries and zeroed in to shoot a rat off a fencepost from a hundred yards without thinking. All of these things Bags saw again as he stuffed an extra water bottle down into his drop pouch, but all of it; their desert camouflage and their desert boots, their weapons and ammo pouches; weighty and full, their helmets strapped to their chins and their freshly shaven faces peering out from under their shadow, in Iraq it all looked different somehow. It looked better. Out here was what all the gear was meant for.

They were scheduled for a three-day op: three days and as many nights patrolling the land between Camp Fallujah and the southeastern edge of the city. Their vehicles were prepped with the food and water, and as the sun approached noon Gunny Ulfe pointed toward a row of farmhouses and then led the way.

LT and his crew remained back on the mound, on the radio with Higher. It was the task of each team to fan out and protect their engineer as he tromped up and down the berms. And between LT's mound and the row of houses there were plenty. No different than the dirt farms back in the US, boundaries out here were defined by elevation. Generations of farmers had built and tended these berms, making a network of risen dirt that girded both land and canal.

Gunny marched out in front for a time and then fell back to let Bags and his team move ahead.

As assistant team leader, it was customary for Jim to take the rear. This stemmed from old Recon lore when their forefathers patrolled in claustrophobic files under the canopies of Vietnam. Bags's team, though, had formed rules all their own. Point men never held the machine gun, but Grass did. His SAW with its snub nose barrel walked out in front. Behind him went their engineer; shoulder to shoulder with Murray, Jim came next and Bags took up the rear. Jim stopped to look into a weedy canal. Bags caught up and they both looked down.

"See somethin'?" Gunny appeared at their elbow.

"No, Gunny. Just lookin'," Jim said, pulling his eyes from the slow water and back up toward Murray and their engineer.

Despite Gunny's appearance and the harsh power he wielded, he rarely exercised it. He blew out in amusement and told Jim it was best not to daydream. Bags was happy Gunny was with them. This was everyone's first deployment, even LT's. But not Gunny. He'd played an armed role in Kosovo and had been in a grunt unit for the Afghan invasion. Anyone who looked could see in those eyes that in charge of them was a man who'd walked into the inferno, and walked out again.

They continued. Not far were the other teams, and Bags heard one of the guys grousing about how dismal the whole place looked. How it was "boring" and "bleak" and probably a "Haj-infested shit hole." Perhaps one could see it that way, sure, if one chose to. As they walked with their rifles in their hands, Bags looked around at something entirely different.

There were homes on the outskirts of the land; modest huts, colored as sand would if whirling into being out from a mirage. The trees in the area were sparse, sure, making all the grander the green of their splendor. The dirt they now walked on, golden brown, was dirt they'd likely never walk on again, and was the same earth that had nurtured the very Fertile Crescent. Those were days when the Abrahamic religions were born or were learning to crawl. Bags was no scholar but he did remember the book *Arabian Nights*, coming much later, and how it told of tales from ancient days.

They got to the row without being shot at or finding a single cache: two events Bags had secretly hoped for. Gunny pointed them in a new direction and from there they searched new berms for caches. And this was their first day.

And the second.

And the third, until not long after they'd sat for an MRE lunch someone in another team yelled. "We've," an excited voice breathed into a radio, "we've found something." A brother team had been skirting along a berm when suddenly their engineer had stopped. His metal detector had apparently squeaked and squawked and soon the nose of their shovel had dug down and hit metal.

All gathered round. That *something* was a bundle of Russian rocket-propelled grenades, along with about a thousand rounds of 7.62; the ammo of choice for the lurking Mujahideen.

That find would beget many. They'd apparently stumbled onto a treasure trove. As Gunny relayed to LT to get the EOD guys on site, the teams spread out to find caches of their own. And they did, one after the other. Their engineer's detectors squeaked with a high pitch and afterwards many lethal finds were dug up: rifles, mortars, more rocket-propelled grenades, a box of blasting caps that numbered in the thousands, and even an old Russian drop bomb so big and bulbous it looked right out of a video game. Bags and his team followed their treasure hunter, marking discoveries with pink survey flags and calling into LT their ten-digit grid.

They followed over new berms and through thickets of reeds that grew out from canals along their path. They crossed a flimsy bridge somewhere and passed two more tractors. They followed until the other teams were but distant calls and new farmlands peeked out from around the lip of a fallen wall.

"Say," Jim scratched his chin as if remembering. "Shouldn't we be stickin' a little closer to Gunny?"

"What's wrong?" Grass said, fondling a pink survey flag. "Scared to be alone?"

Murray trotted up, wiping the sweat from his brow. "Engineer found another," he said. "I'll call it in."

Bags looked. Their engineer was a good distance down their berm now, nearly a stick figure in front of a yellow wall of reeds. "Jim may have a point, we—"

"You're both scared of the *Azzies*!" Grass said.

As if summoned, right then there was a sound: a fierce rushing noise.

Then came a toppling sound, and then there was nothing but an eruption of earth.

A mortar had exploded between them and their engineer.

"Incoming!" Bags cried. He hit the dirt, face first, grappling with his rifle underneath him. Out in the open, there were few choices, but Grass flew down into the canal. Jim ran toward Bags, remembering at the last second their dispersion training, speeding past to dive face-first himself into his own patch of ground. Murray, seeing this, ran the opposite way; toward the smoking impact crater and their frozen engineer.

Another toppling *woo-woo-woop* and dirt roared up, ripped free as if by a clawed hand. It sent Murray and the engineer toppling into Grass's canal. Murray frantically grabbed for his handset.

"Murray!" Bags cried. "You calling it in?"

"Yeah!"

Jim popped up like a gopher. "Gunny's gotta hear this!" He ducked as another impacted, this one far behind them. Soon another fell, but in front of them now.

"They're bracketing!" Bags yelled out. "Let's move— now!" He wasn't sure who'd heard. Whether they were prompted by his words or by seeing him flee, they all, even the engineer, got up and ran.

They ran as a single file. Bags upfront and Jim behind, cursing wildly about trying to spot a forward observer. Behind Jim ran Grass, who looked down with a light in his eyes. Covering the rear now was Murray, pushing the engineer who could not run as they could, for his rifle sling and metal detector had wrapped around him in one big mess.

They knew they were running back toward Gunny. They ran and breathed so hard it was difficult to tell if it was mortar impacts that followed them or the sound of their heartbeats. After a time they came to a lone farmhouse that was surrounded by trees. Bags had his men take cover behind its far wall, joining them and looking toward the horizon for any signs of their platoon sergeant.

Bags turned to Murray. "Did you...did you," he could hardly catch his breath. "Did you make contact?"

"I did," Murray said, panting just as badly. "It was hard to tell. Sounded like Gunny was trying to get some air."

By air, Murray meant aircraft.

"Is that what those things are?" The engineer spoke at last, pointing up at two helicopters.

"Apaches!" cried Grass. "Those are Apaches."

They all watched the attack helicopters approach and then fly past. It had to have been the Alzilal. The mortars were sudden, and close, and what was more Bags could feel it in his bones. They all stood, dripping with anticipation as the helos hunted further and further away. They waited to hear them open up on a target, but it never came.

"Dilute into the farmlands like shadows," Jim eventually said. "I didn't see no forward observer."

"I didn't look," laughed Murray.

Bags sucked from his water bottle, wiping his sweat, saying, "I looked. I didn't see an FO either."

"Well at any rate," Grass now held open a pack of cigarettes, "we're gettin' some war!"

They were covered in dirt, mud, sweat, and sand. They'd made it out alive, much more alive. Wherever their foe was, those pricks wouldn't be loading any tubes with Apaches overhead. Bags prepared for the march back, but not before starting what would become a ritual. He said "Why not?" and sucked on the brown filter as Grass lit his smoke. Bags was not a smoker, but he inhaled and blew it out. Nicotine raced through his brain, so much so that he soon swayed about and almost fell.

There was a day back in Florida, when Bags was about ten or so, back when he was just Tyler and he and his family had gone to the River. They had a cabin there and visited a few times each year. From a single spring, snaked this waterway; through wetlands and pine forests until emptying into the mighty St. Johns. A cool clear ribbon of God's own joy: lily pads on top and swamp cabbage sprouting from its clean dark bottom. The River was Tyler's favorite place in all the world.

Of all the friends he'd invited, only a handful of parents allowed their darlings to run the risk of poison ivy or snakes. Though their ancestors had weathered far worse conditions and far bigger fangs, a time had apparently come when the wonders of the world had begun to lose their luster. Two buddies had made it, though.

The three of them were canoeing; all of them in one big fiberglass monster. Tyler had taken the rear and steered them further away from the family cabin. The boys could still see the dock when the clouds rolled in. But before they could bait a hook or cast a line, a black storm broke out. By the time they'd gotten halfway back, the rain was pulverizing the river with such force they could no longer see the dock. Everything was chaos, jumping and roaring. Trees blew and there was a muffled but horrendous snapping of a trunk somewhere deep in the woods. They knew the dock was there; the river was more or less a straight line. Yet even the trees on the shore were a blur. They paddled onward, and his buddy seated in the middle bailed rainwater as the first piece of hail came down.

One, then another, then a million it seemed; the tiny white artillery cracked off the canoe, their working black paddles, the guy up front's big blond head.

When they got to the dock the hail storm was raging and Tyler's mother was yelling from the refuge of the open door to come inside the cabin and hide. And for a time they did, until the boys, sopping and shaking, looked at each other and ran back out like wild hellions. Tyler's mother screamed but it was no use and she shut the door. The boys, dashing about and avoiding the "big ones," yelled to one another what fun their other friends were missing.

The buzz wore off, and Tyler was now Bags once more, and he tossed his cigarette and they all got moving. The sound of the Apaches was gone and platoon mates could be seen; excited faces poking over a distant berm like rows of cabbage.

"Congratulations," Gunny said as the team went up and over. Now they could see the low mound crowned by all their vehicles. They'd zigzagged in the pursuit of their caches so that they'd gotten disoriented. Bags noted this issue as Gunny said; "First in the battalion to get shot at. LT's on the horn now. That was the Alzilal y'all ran into."

"More like ran away from," Jim said.

"Did those Apaches see anything?" Bags asked.

"Nope." Gunny then gave them all a look, one, that as much as the mortars themselves, told Bags they were all officially in a combat zone. "They just disappeared."

"Like shadows, Gunny," Murray blew out a snort and shook his head.

And like that they were back on the mound, back inside the ring of Humvees and inside their temp' headquarters. LT proudly greeted them and settled things on the radio with

EOD. All the caches they found were annihilated; blown to bits with state-sanctioned C4. Then they packed up and drove back to Camp Fallujah, all the while looking out of windows or from the airy height of a turret; looking for men eyeing their convoy with ill designs. They had all tromped around the farmlands the same, ran for their lives the same, but weariness claimed Bags like no one else. He chalked it up to the weight of duty, like fathers who peter out at the end of a road trip, one whose success or failure landed ultimately on him. And there were many more "road trips." Seven months' worth.

Back at camp, some trailers had been converted into group bathrooms: toilet stalls and showers and a row of urinals bolted to a wall. Bags showered and after crunched gravel with his wet flip-flops and was soon welcomed again by the coolness of his pod. There was mail waiting for him, on his bed; a few white envelopes from the States that must've been sent out before Battalion had even left. Jim had gotten them from the platoon office, he said, after having put fuel in the Humvee.

The letters would have to wait. Bags's duties as a team leader, Marine, or a conscious man would have to wait, too. He slid the letters aside, sunk into his bed and fell quickly asleep.

Tyler didn't enjoy fighting, and he didn't want to lead.

At the River, there was no fighting, and there was no leader. There, amongst the cool mud, rich and black, some canoed in the waters, others fished, some sat out on the dock and drank tea; talking about how long ago a twelve-pound bass got its jaws ripped out by a twelve-year-old whose name no one could remember. Everyone was the master of their fate; the sole, happy composer.

On such a day, bright and hot, Tyler's grandparents drank their tea on the dock. They both had lived through the Depression and had grown up in the same California town. Married at eighteen, his grandad had fought in WWII and his grandmother for a time worked in an aircraft factory just like Marilyn Monroe. Then he came back and she got pregnant. Later, together, they did the opposite of their own grandparents and moved back east, settling in Florida where they built their life and had a slew of kids. Their own children were never able to stay married, and one weekend when Tyler's mother had custody of him, she and her parents packed him up for a full day at the River.

The women sat on the dock in their lawn chairs. Tyler adventured about in the lily pads with a face mask. Grandpa, though usually right in there with him, had crawled out to join the ladies.

No other grandfathers climbed the river trees with the youngsters. And even if one had dared, Tyler doubted they would have jumped off wobbly branches to scare alligators like his did. Those alligators were the "manageable gators," Grandpa had always said. The bigger ones: no way would he jump in or let Tyler go near them, save for a wilderness class about predators who hunted upon the water's surface. Seated on his granddad's knee he learned much; how to bait a hook, what plants he could eat and what their names were, which clouds meant lighting and which ones were "just talk," how to clean fish, how the skinny head on that water snake over there meant it wasn't poisonous because it meant it didn't have any venom glands. And while Tyler learned the Florida variant of manhood, all the while his granddad's tough hand rested on his shoulder, or patted him on his head.

Grandpa was sitting up on the dock, then he made a noise. He grabbed the white hairs on his chest, and then, before the ambulance could arrive down the old dirt road or his mother could rip her own mother's hands from his face, he laid down on the dock and died.

It was night and Bags was seated on his low bed, legs crossed, headlamp on. The headlamps Battalion used had yellow-and-black straps with a lone light dead center the brow line. You could have ones that shined white or red, but in a war zone most burned only blue. Blue was the best for observing blood in the darkness, and in the darkness Bags wrote a letter; filling their room with that soft blue light as Jim snored.

Bags was writing back to his ailing grandma. He told her many things, going into the weather mostly. How it wasn't nearly as hot as he'd expected and that plenty of days in Florida were worse. He told her not to worry, that Iraq wasn't as crazy as the TV made it sound. He stopped writing so he could think, and he thought about his granddad until he wrote another few lines about how, even though he appreciated her kind words, Grandpa was the only hero in the family: her late husband, who stormed the beaches of Normandy.

He put the letter in an envelope and sealed it. He turned off his headlamp and the room again was full of that warm welcoming darkness. As he listened to Jim he remembered how the old man had looked that day on the dock, that day when he stopped breathing. Bags stretched out on his bed and wondered if his grandpa's soul had soared right then to Heaven. And he envisioned such a journey; though he knew he was far from ready to take it.

Tyler's grandfather wasn't the only one in the family who'd served in the military.

Tyler's dad used to be a big surfer. As a teen, his dad couldn't be separated from his single-fin, haunting the Florida east coast from Sebastian to Daytona, with buddies who'd all owned the same Winnebago. But by twenty-five, he never picked up a board again. He'd talk about the surfing when he drank. The big waves, the shark that almost got him off Cocoa Beach when a thunderstorm had rolled through. He talked about surfing, but he never talked about Vietnam.

Tyler's dad had been drafted into the Army. As far as Tyler could tell, he'd been given some support role where he rotted tediously behind the wire until he finally came home with medals he never wore for a war he'd never really fought in. What wrecked his father was not PTSD, for that is perceived as trauma; romantically incurred during battle. Tyler's dad's war was the one waiting for him when he returned.

Planted on the couch. Face in his hands out on the back patio. His dad said it all moved so slow: the traffic, traffic lights, the asses on escalators that didn't budge, the bad Seinfeld jokes. What he needed was something that was no longer there. And if only here, Tyler grew to understand his father. And the traffic his dad fought to the job he hated to pay for the crime of a home he couldn't afford slowly ate him, sentencing him to a life that swallowed him whole.

Tyler's crime was being born in a time and place where dreams had committed suicide. All about him, people in his life drank and smoked and snorted, injected, slogged hopelessly to and from work, past churches where few went. His prison cell: a three-bedroom house where nobody laughed and everyone cried. Then the prison split like a tree in Nam hit by lightning; becoming apartments that he and his sister would bounce between until he turned eighteen and was gone.

Tyler was not, what some would call, a stereotypical Marine.

He wasn't 250lbs of life-taking-heart-breaking muscle. His head and face didn't make him look like a bulldog, nor had he climbed out of the womb waving the red, white, and blue. He hadn't attended a single Fourth of July parade back when he was a teenager. He was just too busy doing kickflips and ollies and spiking his wobbly mohawk to plunge into the pits of Rollins Band, Circle Jerks, U.S. Bombs, and saw Danzig so many times at the House of Blues he could still rank the shows by how hard people went off when Glenn ended things with "Twist of Cain." Tyler had been the kid who didn't make the football team. He skateboarded and flirted with the idea of a lip ring. He held no interest in the JROTC, but then one day the Twin Towers and the Pentagon were attacked, and some strange voice deep inside of him began to speak, and when it started it didn't stop, growing into a scream until he stood on the yellow footprints of Parris Island with his life signed away.

Paroled into the arms of the Marines Corps, Tyler's mind was still polluted by the junk of teenage tribulation—school bathroom fistfights, his father drunk, overdoses, divorce papers, cigarettes smoldering in the living room—yet he soon found his tribe. Put under the charge of three drill instructors: the little one, white; the medium one, Hispanic; and the gargantuan senior DI, black as midnight. All of whom expressed their strange love for the Corps by their insistence the piece-of-shit recruits they were cursed to train would become the finest killers to ever walk the earth.

The DI's uniforms were perfect. Tyler—or now Recruit Boggs—with his shaved head and a persistent cough known as "recruit crud," eyed their chests every chance he could. Most of their ribbons were the same: National Defense Service, Sea Service, Navy Achievement, and Good Conduct—that last one especially surprising to the recruits who pissed their pants when these men screamed in their ear, neck veins bulging.

The DI's were absolute athletes. It was a strange thing, a year or so after boot camp, when it became the norm to rag on the boot camp days. "Those DIs had no war on their chest!" someone would say. Iraq hadn't kicked off yet and only a trim few had seen the mountains of Afghanistan. "They were POGs!" someone else would declare: especially pejorative, as it always came from the frothing mouth of a fellow infantryman. "They were pussies..." And that was the one that Tyler couldn't even pretend to agree with. His three, ranging from about five-foot-six to six-four, were built like statues. The small white one—the drill buff—ran up and down the lines from sun up to sun down. If a recruit dared a sideways glance, one could see the maniac had gray hair; silver shimmering under his broad campaign cover. And he outpaced eighteen-year-olds. That kill hat could do over thirty dead hang pull-ups: a feat he used to shame the "fat bodies" with after watching their dismal two or three. And then of course the senior drill instructor was Lucifer. His thighs were wider than Tyler's waist was round, and his chest was the size of the stump Tyler's grandad had used when he chopped firewood.

And the DIs loved what they did. You had to, to work sixteen-hour days, six or sometimes seven days a week. They yelled so that the flesh of their throat was forever raw: the famous "frog voice" that came with them when they hung up the campaign cover and returned to the fleet.

Tyler drilled on the parade deck. He suffered sand fleas and ruck marches so heavy he felt as if his spine was going to grind itself down to a sick-white, four-inch pulp. He ran, and he did sit-ups, and he did pull-ups; never matching his kill hats but getting twenty-one; one over what allowed them max score on their Personal Fitness Test. He was taught how to shoot and he was taught by his DIs how to clean his weapon and the larger-than-life legends of the Corps. There was Dan Daly, and Smedley Butler, and the godlike Chesty Puller, whom they said goodnight to each time they lay their weary bodies to sleep.

And then one day, with both Tyler's parents and sister somewhere watching in the hushed crowd, Tyler became Private Boggs. He, along with the rest of his recruit training platoon were given their Eagle, Globe, and Anchor: becoming Marines.

Brand new Marines are allowed a week of what is called recruiter's assistance. It's an extra week back home, where you meet your old recruiter in the office he or she recruited you from and assist in whatever task they may have for you. More charismatic newbies have been known to pull in up to half a dozen signatures. Most file paperwork and go home early. It's an extra week to see one's buddies again, to maybe see the old girlfriend and hold on for a bit longer, to walk into your old high school to go see your teacher who was a tanker in Desert Storm and tell him what the hell you've been up to. Tyler did none of those things. Forgoing recruiter's assistance, a week out of boot leave he was sent to the School of Infantry.

Boot camp was where civilian putty was molded into Marines. SOI was where boot Marines learned how to be infantrymen—grunts, the grizzly backbone of the Corps. It was here where he met Private James, already called Jim by the SOI cadre. Jim had gone on recruiter's assistance, and of course that round plucky face had bagged another for Chesty Puller and his beloved Corps. In SOI, in the swampy training grounds of Camp Geiger, not only did Bags and Jim become the best of friends, but together they learned crew-served weapons, how to properly throw grenades, and survived ruck marches that could have broken a mule.

Toward the end of their training, a man walked into their squad bay. The SOI instructors said they had a visitor and told them to gather round. This visitor had gold jump wings and a gold dive bubble pinned on his chest. He said he was Gunnery Sergeant Ulfe, and that he'd just returned to North Carolina from a deployment to Afghanistan with the grunts—"the same murder machines as you gents." But he was now back home, with Marine Recon, and he was currently in charge of the Screening. They were to hold tryouts, and anyone listening had the right to attend. It wouldn't be hard: a PFT of pull-ups and sit-ups and an early morning three-mile run. After came the pool, though, where most failed. "Just show up and give it what you got," Gunny Ulfe said. "Those of you who pass shall come to me, to the Recon Indoctrination Platoon." This platoon, known ominously as RIP, was where the real vetting began.

Of the sixty or so who listened to Gunny speak that day, about twenty signed up.

Private T. Boggs and Private T. James were two names on that list, and those names were soon read aloud as they and the other hopefuls departed the warmth of a bus to stand nervous and cold in a field in Camp Lejeune in the pre-dawn morning.

Camp Lejeune was next to Camp Geiger, and the whole ride there the bus had been alive with whispers. Some were chomping at the bit. Some regretted their decision and knew if they hadn't signed up for this adventure they'd still be sleeping in the racks back at SOI. Bags and Jim were somewhere in the middle, seated next to the other and saying nothing.

They stood at some distance from the other, out in the darkness. The twenty had been lined up alphabetically in front of the pull-up bars and the screening had begun. A dim figure with a clipboard revealed itself to be Gunny Ulfe. Around him were other figures, and as "Private Boggs, you're up" mounted the bar he couldn't help but see that they were fit like his DIs, but in some ways radically different.

For Marines, these guys had shaggy hair. He'd expected a super gung-ho type. He'd heard about Recon since boot camp; the ninjas of the Corps. If merit begat station in the Marines, which was stated constantly, and high-and-tight haircuts mixed with hoarse throats meant merit, which had been his Marine Corps world thus far, then who were these tattooed and intense, but eerily laid-back dudes? Hell, a couple looked better fit for a Rollins Band mosh pit than marching around on a parade deck.

Tyler knocked out his twenty and from there the sun broke over the trees. The PFT was like all the others, lonely and grueling. Even on an early-morning tank trail, surrounded by men striving for the exact purpose as you are, you run alone.

Once they were bused to the pool on the other side of Camp Lejeune, loneliness became impossible. It was hard to feel by one's self when the hands and feet of a panicked slew caught your cammies and pulled you gurgling halfway to the bottom. Somewhere in the ruckus he caught a glimpse of Jim. His face was red and his eyes looked like a startled horse, rolling this way and that for an escape from the confined water tread.

In the end, seven made it. SOI soon ended and they were cut orders to Battalion and then put in the hands of Gunny Ulfe.

Gunny would leave RIP, as would Bags and Jim. But first, the two had to go through what was until then the hardest era of their lives, all in preparation for ARS—the Amphibious Reconnaissance School—purportedly the hardest school in the Corps.

Boot camp and SOI had early mornings, but in RIP a determined group of twelve were in formation when not a bird sang. The other five had passed the screening before them and deemed themselves elder statesmen, just under the cadre themselves in all manner of seniority and instruction. From these formations would begin their morning training; long, fast, punitive runs that in one go were equal to or greater than the miles covered in two weeks back in Parris Island.

Physical training was the very heart of RIP. Not only the runs but the pull-ups, flutter kicks, a thing called "zero push-ups" were a particularly punk-rock staffer delighted in taking lead. "Remember." he'd say, "It's not you versus the numbers. It's you versus yourselves." They would do their prescribed pushes, always yelling "zero," no matter how high the actual count rose. Then, of course, there was the pool, and its meaner cousin the salty ocean off Onslow Beach. Jim always straggled behind on the swims; caught in his gear or swimming slug-gishly when they were afforded the fortune to go slick. With Jim always would be Gunny, telling him in a fatherly voice all he had to do was quit.

After some weeks it struck Bags that Gunny was using RIP to drape himself once more in that community. A platoon sergeant in a grunt unit was not the same as being senior en-listed in a battalion where men reportedly worked in much smaller groups. When not panting at the end of a ten-mile run or trying not to get pulled under in the base pool, the twelve students—Ropes, called such for the rope they wore—listened as Gunny told them what pain and glory awaited those who made it through.

The rope they wore like a sash was tied to their heritage, running all the way back to WWII. It was a repelling rope, and the knots each Rope had to learn had allowed warriors down cliffs, kept them strapped to god only knew what aircraft, and of these knots seasoned Recon Marines could and would test them. Far more fitting for the beating heart of a young warlike man was the trigger time. Recon was a haven for shooters, gunslingers; Marines who'd spend more time on the ranges and shoot houses than anyone in the Corps. And if they weren't kicking in doors, they may find themselves on their bellies under deep brush, carrying on their most noted tradition. Surveillance was, above all, the reason for their being. They were to master communication, observation, and various reports; ranging from detailing the bend in a road to determining the depth of an enemy lagoon. But it wasn't radios or binoculars that lit a fire in Tyler's eye, it was what Gunny said about how they'd get there.

The jump wings and dive bubble the cadre all wore were not for show. For those who crawled through the furnace of ARS and came out the other side signed, brand-new recondos, jump and dive school bestowed upon them the skills of Insert.

Insert...and Extract; two ever-important words. Gunny nurtured their young minds to see the life that awaited them was one where Marines worked in small teams, often close to or behind enemy lines. They had to rely on one another without doubt, and getting in and out of hostile territory was as important to their mission as the mission itself.

Jumping out of planes to fight alongside like-minded men —feeling the bliss of falling in action: Tyler found new inspiration for their deathly morning runs. Soon they were packed up once more and sent to ARS.

Much could be told of that old school. Much would be a retelling of RIP. All they had trained their minds and bodies for was tested and then some, and four months later Private First Class Boggs and Private First Class James returned to Battalion as its newest official members.

There were times, Tyler had to admit, when inside a good

skate park a type of steel-eyed determination would shadow the face of a guy. It would be when someone bloodied by a high ramp, at the top of it, bound to try again. Something about the skater's stance would shift. Something about the look in the skater's eye said "I conquer this, or it conquers me." The kid no longer feared embarrassment or pain. He only felt, as the future Marine felt, the white-hot will toward winning.

Being in a recon battalion was to be surrounded by such men. Whether cutting down their run time for the next PFT, whether it be improving their shot group or memorizing the uses for the metric ton of gear they were issued, here was a land where dreams were alive. It was not grandiose to suggest, for a few beers in and many would confess their love at the thought of chiseling their names into the stone of legend.

Tyler wasn't so sure about fame when he and Jim were sent to jump school. He enjoyed the company and challenge far more than the thought of glory. That company he especially missed, for jump school was held at Fort Benning. For three weeks he was denied his barracks room and new friends, though at least he got five falls from a plane.

Jump-qualified and glowing, they returned to Lejeune to learn that their newest skill would be put to immediate use. The following morning Battalion had a series of jumps planned. These would be out of helicopters; a far more thrilling venture, for one just simply ran out the back to be greeted by the sun.

And along the way, their team leader, a senior corporal who had pushed with the Iraq invasion, on his way down to meet LZ Bluebird landed badly and broke both ankles.

Murray and Grass had just graduated ARS. Only a day

back to Battalion, they were too green to jump alongside the rest of their team. Their team was Bags and Jim and a senior corporal who was told in the hospital that he would be out a deployment and possibly was looking at medical retirement.

"Boggs," Gunny Ulfe said, poking his head out of the platoon office.

Bags knew what that meant, and he trotted in to find not only Gunny Ulfe but LT. Both looked somber.

"Gunny? Sir?"

"We want you to be Team Leader."

Bags gaped as he would at a firing squad. "Gunny—Sir," he said, feeling his palms go sweaty behind him as he tried to maintain parade rest. "I think James wants it," he lied. "He's senior," which wasn't a lie; Jim had gone to boot camp a week earlier, picked up rank a smidge quicker due to having nabbed that new recruit for the almighty Corps.

But these meant nothing to recon men. "Jim's solid as stone," said Gunny. There was a twinkle in his eye, belying genuine warmth. "But you have a way of thinking for yourself, don't you? We've seen it. Any other unit, your higher-ups would be cursing your DIs for not beating the civilian out of you. But here, and where we're soon going, thinking outside the box may be more needed than anything else. If LT here goes down, if *I* go down, we've agreed that we want TLs who'll do things their own way."

Bags would have hidden in Gunny's dip bottle if it meant getting out of this. He set his face to stone, making small nods of defeat as his leaders then nailed his coffin shut. In typical Marine Corps fashion, they criticize-complimented him on how his PFT score was good but could be better, how his uniform rarely looked like shit, how he handled weapons well enough so they weren't worried about getting blasted in the head while on patrol from a negligent discharge…and that he should, and better, look at this as the honor that it was.

Bags accepted. He had no choice. He left the platoon office wanting only two things; to not be Team Leader and to curse his former one's parents for giving him such weak bones. He wanted a third thing; to jump from another helicopter with no chute and land squarely on his head.

And yet here Bags led. The platoon was at present back outside the wire and all over the farmlands, this time close enough to the Euphrates to see her rushing blue. The team had been walking next to an aqueduct, one of those above-ground ones that were a few feet off the earth like one big endless feeding trough. The field that Murray and Grass, and Jim and Bags walked amongst was a vibrant green. Jim wondered out loud what plant sprouted from the soil, and no one could answer. It was as if they patrolled through high neon, surprised when they found themselves avoiding crushing a particular blade with their muddy boots. They walked with the aqueduct to their right; its silver shining in the midday sun as a thicket of date palms drew near.

Behind the trees waited another berm. This was to be the last for the day. For weeks they'd found caches; so many that their finds started to dry up. These last two days had been one big continuous nothing. Another team had found a small cache of AK-47s right out the gate, then nothing. EOD had taunted them that their truck was way too full. Normally, by day two, the skies would smoke with the aftermath of controlled detonations. By day three, having found zilch, Bags couldn't help but wonder if they'd worked themselves out of a job.

"Engineer's found something!" Murray hollered back. He was out in front with the engineer and Grass ran up beside them. Three digs of the shovel and Grass exposed the first buried mortar. There were many more.

"Go ahead and call it in, Murr'," Bags said.

"Radio's been giving me shit all day." Murray shook his handset. "But I'll try."

"Jim," Bags him aside. "Make sure Murray packs a spare battery next time."

Jim nodded and said he understood. As the men got digging and the radio got working, their team uncovered one of the biggest arsenals the Marines had seen. EOD was put to work, rolling up in their Humvee along with Gunny and LT. LT had brought extra shovels and always insisted he dig alongside his men. Gunny remained by their vehicle, monitoring the radio with a perturbed look on his face.

More and more enemy munitions came out of the ground. Grass and Jim and the engineer took care to stack them in little pyramids. These were the best for EOD, who set to work rigging the mounds with just the right amount of C-4. Under the date palms it was a veritable beehive: marines digging, others stacking, others pulling security while EOD techs rolled out detonation cord while Gunny watched on with a pale face.

By late afternoon, the whole platoon had gathered. After the guys were moved to a safe distance and the last blasting cap was stuck into the awaiting plastic explosive, enemy-held death and mayhem went up in one instant with a string of annihilation. The Marines used to cheer for the ringed flumes of smoke trailing in the air like spirits, the thundering tremor that ran up your legs if the cache had been particularly big. Today, though, the Marines watched in silence.

"Well," Gunny called out to everyone. "That does it."

"Does what?" someone asked.

"This last one," Gunny answered, "put us over the top. Higher says we've rid the enemy of more weaponry than any unit thus far in Iraq."

For this, the men did cheer. Would this mean medals? Bags was sure LT was walking over to high-five Gunny, but Gunny dropped his handset to hold his stomach and ran behind a tree.

Murray cleared his throat and read the paper again, this time making sure he was sounding flamboyant and official. "As of 20 October 2004," he read, "Battalion has uncovered and destroyed…" he held the page like a sacred document, like the torch of the Statue of Liberty perhaps, making the fact that it had been torn off the platoon office's wall all the more amusing.

"Say it again!" slurred Grass, who took another shot of whiskey and then passed the bottle to Jim.

"Wait for it," Murray said, this time eyeing Bags until Bags shook his head and nodded the okay. "Uncovered and destroyed *more enemy ordnance than any other unit in Iraq!*"

And there it was—again. They cheered. They congratulated. They affirmed how effective and awesome they were. They'd partaken in a vast cleanup; a worthy, wartime uncovering; ridding the area so completely that the enemy's cupboard now lay bare and it was time to consider what the heck the next step would be. Stuffed in Jim and Bags's side of the trailer, the four hooted and howled while outside hung a low Iraqi moon.

It felt good, more than good. In the foggy waste of foreign service, to have a tangible goal met was as fair as any medal. A playlist was carrying on from Grass's iPod; a mix of CCR and a whole host of other "at war" music whose cheesiness made them act even more like children.

The boys were drinking. Grass and had seen to it that whiskey had been smuggled all the way past customs in a giant Listerine bottle. Jim was still holding it; working up the courage to take another shot out of its full black cap. Bags, who hadn't taken a shot, was holding a pair of flex cuffs.

"Okay," Bags soon said, not losing his cheer. "Word has it we'll be dealing with detainees soon."

"Yeah," Grass blurted. "Who's gonna be the one to get wrestled down by a hundred-pound Iraqi?"

Bags tossed him the cuffs. "I'm so very glad you ask." Bags then held up his desert boonie cover. Boonies, the flimsy cowboy hats of the Corps; great for protecting the head and neck from a relentless sun while out in the field. They were also good for drawing names. Bags grabbed a piece of paper and wrote down *Bags, Grass, Murr, Big Jim*, then he tore the four pieces off the page, folded them, and dropped them into his hat. He grinned and gave it a good, ceremonial shake.

The rules: two names drawn, two men in the ring—or the floor, rather. The first name was given the flex cuffs. The second would be the stand-in for a wily Iraqi, hell-bent on not being detained. A timer was set for a furious sixty seconds. Whoever lost, be it because they couldn't get the cuffs around their opponent's wrists or from succumbing to that very dev-ice…to the whiskey they went.

And names were read. Over and over.

Murray and Grass were the first to go; a stalemate, resul-ting in Murray taking a shot. It was quickly visible how much easier it was to be the resister, and Bags's cackle clued everyone in that their team leader had well considered this. More names were drawn and a blur of matches commenced.

Murray and Grass were bigger than Bags, though Bags had a scrappiness that shined; seizing a neck or sweeping out from under his foes their arm with a fast, hilarious kick. Poor Jim, though, was a lamb for the slaughter. Short in stature and in reach, Grass and especially Murray balled him up and cuffed him, even if they were supposed to be playing Iraqi; sending him again and again to the bottle.

Before long a pool of sweat gleamed from the trailer floor. Grass stood shirtless with his hands on his hips, breathing hard and smiling harder. Jim looked like he was about to fall over. And Murray was crouching wrestler-low and gave Bags the "come on"—because their names had been drawn.

Bags squeezed the cuffs in his hand. He squared his stance and bounced light on his feet, knowing that he and Murr' looked like fighters in a low-grade Octagon. Murray held a goofy smile and eyes intent, and Bags knew he was going to resist with a tackle and then afterward work his way to mount. It's what he'd been doing all night to both Grass and Jim. The-re he'd sit on Bags and wrestle for the flex cuffs until Grass yelled "Time!"

But not if Bags could shoot in first.

He darted, flying under Murray's arms and knocking himself near senseless against one of Murray's knees. But he'd done it! He jammed his head between Murray's legs and wrapped his arms around his calves and bulled forward, upending the rat bastard until Murray's back hit flat on the floor.

"Who's in mount now?" Bags growl-laughed as Grass cheered and Jim ran outside to puke. The team leader had mitigated his opponent's bicycle kicks and now sat on his stomach. "Get in there," Bags growled. He had a hand by the wrist, working one loop of the cuff over those defiantly splayed-out fingers. "Hah!" He'd done it; cinching the cuff tight and looking down at Murray with the determined eye of victory.

"Not today!" Murray cried. Seizing Bags's with his free hand, Murray spun at full speed, flipping Bags onto his back, going along with him until he rested on top.

Bags tried, but Murray's efficiency in freeing himself was commendable. In the end, when Grass called time, Bags had been defeated. Both Murray and Jim helped Bags up, though Jim had tossed his cookies and was professing he was more than fine.

Grass held the Listerine bottle in one hand, its laden cap in the other. "For you, my good sir," he gloated.

"Yeah, yeah." Bags took the cap, looking at its content and taking a breath. The liquor went down his throat like syrupy fire. Training was over and Grass was happy to pour him another. Bags then sat on the floor. Grass and Murr' confirmed Jim was going to make it, and talk turned to different things.

The swimmy feeling in Bags's head always made him think about his baby sister. A couple shots of whiskey were one thing, opioids though...what had wrecked her mind? And if it wasn't pills it had been crack; the street go-to when the sly doctor offices began being raided back when Bags was still only Tyler. Did she choose to turn out that way: a drug addict? Tyler supposed, yes, she did, as the skydiver chooses to jump, as the American chooses to serve, as the Iraqi chooses to fight him. From all these the human puppet is pulled by the strings of their birth. Jam us somewhere, at a certain time, coded with certain genes and dispositions, we won't be able to help ourselves, we will react.

Sure, we know the danger, we tell ourselves we won't do it forever, we jot down marks on calendars saying no more, but we always find excuses to jump, to serve, to fight, to use...to react.

His sister had started life blonde-haired and bright-eyed. But by fourteen, right around the time Tyler was taking off for boot camp, it was like that lens that covers a crocodile's eyes grew out from her skull to suddenly slide down and veil her forever. When Tyler came back on boot leave, he saw how truly different she'd become. No longer was there the tomboy. In her place was a withdrawn, moody Gollum. Attempts at explaining it away as just adolescence soon ended when their mother found the first bag of pills.

What came next were the talks, then chasing much older boys out of the yard or yelling at their ass-end as they scampered out of her window.

"The search for male approval," or something someone somewhere once said when Tyler pondered about it all out loud. Her fall began at the feet of their father. Or his emotional absence, more like. It was true that their dad had always paid his bills. Never once did they starve or lack clothing or the ability to go to a summer camp with a jazzed-up name. Material needs were met but their father was just simply never there.

Tyler read many years later a book about the absent father/ devouring mother duo, and how it allegedly breeds self-destructive children. Tyler and his dad at least had the beach. Though the old man no longer surfed, he did add to Bags's grandfather's lessons and taught him a thing or two about fishing; bait, secret sweet spots, where to throw a line at the mangroves to hook the best snapper. Around the time his sister would have been old enough to join them, those beach trips ended. There were no explanations, no mark on the calendar. The tires just never met the sand anymore, and their dad's drinking got worse.

One night, Tyler's mom called the police. Cops came and told a brood of miscreants that they'd be arrested if they ever stepped foot on the property again. A week after that night came the house-to-house searches. These became necessary when his sister hadn't been heard from in a day or two. She'd once brought over other zombie-eyed girls, and the ones who still lived weren't too far away.

Then there came the sad attempts at interventions. There was a weekend stay in a state-funded detox center. There were prayers and consults with preachers. Then there was an overdose of another teenager nearby, one Bags had known since she was placed in her crib.

Then came the late-night searches. These were reserved for when no one had heard from her in a long, agonizing stretch; gaps of time when Tyler's parents would come together to divide the labor of driving through bad neighborhoods and waiting by a house phone for the cops to call. One such neighborhood Tyler remembered with vivid clarity. He had been home on Christmas leave, the leave before he went up to ARS. His mom had said they'd once found her here and the thought of why repulsed him so thoroughly he almost threw up. He insisted he drive, and with his mother calling out turns it was like looking at a social experiment gone horribly wrong. Terribly so. Streetlights were busted. Trash lay everywhere. Those milling about were shadows; ducking in and out of buildings with condemned signs. The few whom Tyler could make out all looked like the undead from some video game. He noticed how his mother didn't wince when these addicts approached their car. She'd seen them before. Tyler turned on the wipers when it began to rain. He wished the rain would wash it all away; the filth on the windshield, the filth on the streets, the filth that had spewed from his mouth just moments earlier toward his own mother, screaming about how could she and Dad be so mired in their own self-pity that they allowed this to happen. They pulled onto a road with a lone streetlight blinking at the far end. Under it was a small figure. As they approached, it became who they'd been looking for, in white high heels, maybe ninety pounds, standing in the rain.

Mortars came raining in, pulling Tyler out of his thoughts. "Yo!" Murray was snapping his fingers in front of his face. "You in there, Bags? We gotta move!"

Grass was helping Jim into his gear. "The bunker," Ty— Bags said, coming off of the floor and seizing his flak jacket. His Kevlar went on next, then after he was holding his rifle, telling Grass and Murray to meet them outside.

Armed and armored, the four crawled into a bunker. It was a concrete cave with an open backend, just spacious enough to take a high-knee. Such caves were placed strategically throughout the vast trailer park. Constructed to withstand incoming fire, Bags saw the entire platoon was packed within. The guys nearest him, he could make out well enough. But after their front line, a cluster of black clumps huddled and snickered as more mortars fell.

LT was sitting nose-to-nose with Bags.

"What's on your breath, Boggs?"

"...Listerine, sir." Bags could actually feel Grass and Murray popping gum in their mouths, but not before grabbing Jim and sliding him furtively across the gravel to the outermost edge.

LT eyed them queerly, "Things are *obviously* ramping up," he said. "On top of that, Gunny's sick." The lieutenant talked about gut bugs and the infamous Saddam's Revenge. As he did, the four looked around and peered at the silhouettes until they indeed saw Gunny wasn't there.

A mortar hit a trailer nearby, lighting the night with a violent explosion. Someone's home had just been torn like a tuna can. Through the short tunnel of the bunker, sparks beyond suddenly revealed a man's face.

The scream of that trailer's roof having flowered outward had pulled all their eyes in that direction. Bags and his team now observed a man sitting there, at the far end of the bunker. His legs were crossed and his back was against the concrete. Odd that a man so old would be in there with them, or in a helmet, or in Iraq at all. As the sparks died, they could make out he had a white beard; trimmed up to his face, a face that looked out at the night as if deep in thought.

"Who is that?" Bags whispered to LT.

"Some old fogey," LT croaked, "who writes for a Christian magazine."

Bags squinted. The sparks had all but gone, but someone's flashlight was blazing away over there. Bags nodded. The old man's blue jeans and construction boots and his bare, outdated flak jacket all yelled Civilian. He figured the old-timer was there to write a piece on Camp Fallujah, or something, but the lieutenant wasn't done.

"In fact," LT said, suddenly sounding grave, "he'll be attached to your team, Mr. Listerine."

"B-But," Bags soon stuttered.

"But, sir," Jim sputtered from behind the rest of the team. Grass—good god—the thought of Grass being observed by someone who wrote...*that stuff.*

"But nothing," LT demanded.

"Sir," Bags said. "There may be better teams. That's all. What we mean is we all walk fast on patrol. Not sure that gentleman would be able to keep up. What if—"

Another salvo came in. The concrete shook and sand trickled down onto the gravel. Somewhere out there, someone screamed. Bags turned and looked out from that gaping mouth at the indifference of the stars. Their enemy was giving it to Camp Fallujah. He watched as Jim, whose drunkenness had turned calm and reflective, looked out at a fire growing near the showers.

Jim shook his head, "It's them Alzilal again."

Murray couldn't resist. He rose on his knees, calling out over everyone, "Hey old man, you really want to go out in *this?*" Murray pointed toward the fires, toward the sounds of more screams, toward Fallujah where enemies laid in wait.

Karl Carmichael—who would insist on being referred to not as Karl, or Mr. Carmichael, or *that reporter*, but simply as Carmichael—was too weathered. He'd heard too many sharp things from too many sharper people to let Murray's words mean much. The team was about to get an attachment like no other. Everyone in that bunker turned to watch him give his helmet a good slap. Even in the low light of the fire, they could all see him grin. "You bet," the old man said. "Kind of reminds me of Korea."

Fires must be put out, even long after Fallujah. Years later, after LT told the team they'd be getting Carmichael as an embedded journalist, Tyler sat quietly in full-blown business attire. He was in dark slacks—shoes and belt matching—in a long shirt that was white and collared; all hiding post-deployment tattoos. He leaned his back against a wall, but the wall was not the concrete of a working bunker, but the bland-sterile beige of yet another giant conference room.

It was the second event of its kind, both in the same year. Broadcast far and wide as an enhancer of a healthy work environment, *Employee Sensitivity Training* was full steam ahead, captained by a higher-up from the human resources department. The HR head made the usual rounds: diversity and inclusion and representation and a never-ending, over-flowing goblet of respect for any and all.

And when Tyler's phone started to vibrate it did not stop. Diversity is our strength, he heard. Privilege and something about fragility—he struggled to listen, finally joining the rest of the people in the back row by pulling out his phone.

There was an eruption on Facebook: LT had died in a skiing accident.

Tyler felt a knot immediately tighten in his throat, and he scrolled as the voice up front drove on.

We are like balloons hovering over blades of grass, bounced off of him.

Misgendering is violence, he did not hear.

There were three pics in the Facebook post: all of them already coalescing into a memorial. One was of LT standing in a crater left by a monster mortar. Tyler gulped and knew it was going to be hard to swallow.

The second photo was his old lieutenant in his dress blues. Tyler remembered that one; the Marine Corps ball of 2005. That was when Battalion had been back for just long enough to feel garrison again. That was when the teams had been broken up and new ones were still forming. It was before the Corps had pulled their leaders to new posts, new duties, sprinkling them from Quantico, Virginia to the islands of Japan. Tyler remembered how he and Jim forwent that ball, and how he learned the next day that Grass and Murray had roared into the place howling drunk, and not one officer had cared. He remembered seeing LT that evening before, in those blues, walking from somewhere in the barracks to his car.

The third was LT looking lordly in his cammies and body armor at a vehicle checkpoint. He didn't know who had taken the picture, probably the corpsman or the comm guy. It somehow seemed to capture Iraq in a single frame: a clear blue sky with a helicopter far in the distance, a thin black road running straight then curving behind two buildings; one shot-up and the other having not suffered a single round, vehicles out of frame must have been lined up, waiting their turn, and the car that sat center-frame; a beat-up white and orange taxi, sat parked on the road with its trunk and doors open. Talking to the driver was LT.

Many Iraqis spoke English, and by the looks of this, the young man with the black beard was doing so. There were Marines behind the car. All of them were turned, looking at the shot-up building and Tyler couldn't help but guess they were snickering at the blown-off front door. But LT, he had the composure found in a Renaissance painting. His mouth was open, as if in midspeech. Though his eyes were covered by his sunglasses, one could tell he was looking the other man in the eye. He held his rifle with the solemn duty of a man at war, yet no menace there frowned.

Tyler snapped out of it and came up for a breath.

The HR head was now tapping her hair with a finger, doing a big "thinkkk!" gesture, saying be careful about the potential offense of nicknames. You don't know—you just don't know what violence these nicknames may cause. Tyler retreated back to his phone screen.

He scrolled through the comments next, seeing names and faces he hadn't thought too much about for years. Senior enlisted who were retiring when he'd just first arrived, these men, their profile photos mostly them in their cammie-painted heydays, they posted condolences like "Gone but not forgotten," and "Fair winds and following seas." Then Tyler saw Hendershot, now fat with a beard, who wrote, "Big Ears was the finest officer I ever met in the Corps. RIP, sir." Tyler went back to LT's dress blues and couldn't help but laugh.

"Is something funny?" the HR head asked, crossing *zir* arms.

Tears came down Tyler's face. He wiped them. "No, ma'am—"

The whole company took in a collective gasp. Those nearest creaked their necks, giving him concerned grimaces as they all cringed.

"—I mean," Tyler said. "No."

Tyler slid his iPhone back into his pocket. A fire had been lit in the nicety tyrant's eyes, though he was relatively sure she hadn't seen him doing anything other than look down.

"As I was just saying," she resumed her lecture, turning back to the PowerPoint presentation behind her, but not before first giving Tyler that final eye, "whether you intend to or not, things like misgendering, deadnaming, or assuming that nicknames should be used without expressed and clear permission…all harmful."

"Not as harmful as a 120mm mortar, you stupid intolerable bitch! Not as harmful as harsh days under a relentless sun, or being a hooker out on rain-and-grime streets, not as bad as the mind and body slamming into a damn pine tree going sixty down a fucking slope!"

Tyler wanted to yell all of these, but he did in his head. Occasionally she turned and he caught her glance. The fire in those eyes had cooled, and if the Marine Corps had taught him anything, he knew sometimes it was best just to shut up.

Still, he wondered what sense it made when these people talked about family. The company was "meant to be like a family." What a laugh. Blood was one thing, but families formed outside the household knew one another in and out. In many ways, they were stronger than blood. There were no pretenses, no posturing, no whimsical rules to live by, and nothing forged these relationships like adversity.

His brothers, his family whom he'd sweat for and bled with back in Battalion, there were no insults, no bad nicknames, no words between them that could not be spoken.

Bags ended up facing many so-called families. Shackled down by predictability, routine, companies and their softball teams, a jogger meetup group, ambitious pub crawls, they all proclaimed they were somehow, something *more*. Tyler pitied them. All of them. What hollowing out had occurred in his land that so few parents were married and no one knew their neighbors? So much so a group of strangers who all run together on Wednesdays is a *family*? A tribe?!

The heart and the history books said a sense of belonging came from religions, groups joined by blood, small tribes who all knew and depended on each other. All these new attempts struck him more and more as reactions to escape from what replaced all those time-honored things. The company team and the joggers and the pub crawlers all seemed to be fleeing from loneliness, perhaps purposelessness, definitely long hours of clogged commutes where one's feet never stalk the forest floor but one's ever-fattening ass sat in the driver's seat as strangers eked past. The slowness in which life crawled made Tyler think, from time to time, of LT and how he'd gone out. As years passed, rumors grew. One decided the lieutenant had come back with a horrid case of PTSD, and that alone steered him into that tree. Another suggested that because of his devout Christian upbringing he was therefore a tortured homosexual, one who opted for death rather than disownment from the tribe. Tyler never bought either. As best as he could trace, such rumors arose from men who'd known LT in passing but never served under him directly. It was hard for those who'd survived explosions and hellfire to accept death could come so arbitrarily. Tyler always liked to imagine his former platoon commander on his final slope, alive, very much alive, a smile on his face and maybe the wind in his hair. He wanted to go to the funeral but obligations with the job prohibited him. There was a mandatory team-building exercise, and he was the new guy. Many so-called families.

Late October in Iraq had arrived, and with it the leaflets.

Those who patrolled near Fallujah had heard the broadcasts; terse, repetitive pronouncements, all in Arabic, barking out of giant megaphones attached to Humvees. These told the residents of the city to grab their lives and leave. The leaflets, however, the paper deluge that fell from planes, those came with the messages meant to drive a wedge between the locals and the insurgency. We know you are *different*. Report any insurgents to this-or-that number. For war loomed: the great battle of the era.

The enemy who awaited the Coalition forces, the enemy who dug tunnels and laced the sides of streets with daisy-chained IEDs, many of them were from elsewhere. The highest of the higher-ups had said these diehards came from Syria and Chechnya and from the Saharan heat of the great Sudan. These terrorists had busied themselves not just with instruments of death, but by telling the Iraqi population that American "precision" attacks only killed innocent men and women.

The leaflets that fell also told those in Fallujah who the prior attacks had targeted, and why they had been killed, and that the current nest of insurgents kept the city from receiving humanitarian aid.

Operation Phantom Fury would flood the city, but by then most of its people had taken heed and fled. LT and Gunny had said the platoon would likely be involved with managing the exodus. Even before going wheels up from North Carolina, vehicle checkpoints were something they'd trained for.

It had been a rather hilarious event, back in Lejeune. Iraqi's vehicles wouldn't be Humvees, but beaten, worn out trucks and cars. The solution then was simple: task a few Marines to hop in their F-250s and Daewoos and line up and let their brothers inspect away. More dip cans and knives and porno mags were seized in ten minutes than in your average prison shakedown. Guys rotated duties: over-watch, the men who inspected nothing and stayed on the lookout for trouble; the inspectors, who went through glove compartments and trunks pretending to look for blasting caps and AK-47s; then of course the Iraqi's fleeing, who, by Gunny's directives, occasionally heckled their inspector and needed to be brought to their knees.

Now in Iraq, doing VCPs for real, one such "troublemaker" was brought back up to his feet. Murray had thought he'd spotted the makings of a bomb. Long strands of copper wire ran from the back of a cell phone. Only after Grass had grabbed the little Iraqi and pinned him about twenty feet away, down against the sand, did Murray discover the wires weren't attached to anything and the phone's backing was still in place.

"He didn't do anything," Bags laughed. "Let him go, Grass."

Grass nodded and sent the man on his way. Next to Bags was Carmichael. He was in his blue jeans and his construction boots. His long shirt and beard were as white as the one or two clouds overhead. His flak and helmet: equally green. He was watching the checkpoint unfold, scribbling now and then a note in his notepad.

"You were in Korea?" Bags asked, now watching Jim try to open a trunk.

"Saw Chesty Puller with my own eyes." Carmichael kept his gaze straight, squinting against the sun.

"You were a Marine then?"

"Still am, as they say." The old man turned to Bags and he winked. "Yes, I was. Fought in the Frozen Chosin as an eighteen-year-old Private."

"And you saw Chesty?" Bags laughed.

"Just once. I was knocking the ice off my eyebrows one morning and he just so happened to walk by. He didn't look happy."

The whole platoon was checking vehicles, everyone except Gunny. That poor soul was still emptying his bowels at the cyclic rate back at Camp Fallujah. The little black road that connected Fallujah to god knows where was packed, clogged with a line of idling cars and trucks all patiently waiting. Up front now was a taxi; one of those clown cars where one quarter panel will be white and the other bright orange.

LT was helping with this one while Bags and Carmichael watched a lone helicopter way out in the distance. "It's unfortunate Gunny Ulfe can't be here," Carmichael said. "He's a good man."

Bags had thought on and off all morning how odd it felt; Gunny not being out with them. Bags crinkled his brow. "You know him?"

"Know him?" Carmichael laughed. "I was attached to Ulfe's platoon for the Afghan invasion. We became fast friends. It was he who requested I come out with you, you know. He didn't tell you any of this?"

"No," Bags said. "He probably would have if he—"

"Wasn't sitting on a toilet right now?"

They both chuckled, catching a glance from LT who was busy winning hearts and minds with the taxi driver.

"Yeah," is all Bags said, detaching himself from where they stood to relieve Jim and check some vehicles.

The way they'd set it all up was simple, and usually the same. Though VCPs were intended to scrutinize who was leaving the city, traffic could still come from the other direction. To prevent trouble from rolling in from the farmlands, two Humvees would park and face one another from both sides of the road. These were the Humvees set on the south end; their crew-served weapons facing the vast space where a car never once appeared. This day, the southern Humvees were beyond the road's curve, hidden by buildings that'd already seen a bit of war. The north-end Humvees were set up the exact same, and these were the ones everyone predicted were going to take a hard blast one of these days. Iraqi traffic would crawl up in a cautious train, stopping just before the frowning American vehicles until waved through by Marines to stop short of a row of parking cones. And watching the three or four vehicles as they were inspected was the fifth

Humvee, parked away from the road a good fifty feet; its gunner ready to lay waste to whatever or whomever LT commanded.

"You write for a magazine?" Bags said. It wasn't a question, really. Carmichael was behind him as Bags bent forward and searched under a passenger seat.

"I do," the old man said.

Bags nodded his head. His focus was on his fingers, fiddling around in the nether regions where his eyes couldn't reach. "So, you fought in Korea. Then what? Journalism school or something?"

"No, I'm afraid not. Stayed in."

"Career Marine Corps. You go to Vietnam?"

Bags heard the man's voice change. It was hard to detect but it was there. He sounded as if he were being put to brag but didn't wish to do so. Nevertheless, Carmichael said, "For as many tours as men you got in your team, young *Bags*, as they seem to call you."

Bags stood and placed his back against the checked car. The old man was already tall and seemed somehow to be growing taller. Bags caught a twinkle in the corner of his eye.

Bags had encountered the mortar attacks of the Alzilal, but that was all. Here stood a man who'd battled in the colds of Korea. Bags's heart couldn't help but turn to a cadence a DI sung back on Parris Island. In the Marine Corps, a year was a decade, and more than a year had passed. But the song as he remembered it now shouted in his skull:

In the cold of Korea,
Under six feet of snow,

There's a US Marine,
And he's puttin' on a show.

Not only Korea, Carmichael said he'd been a platoon sergeant in Vietnam; leading his own men in that sweltering heat.

In the Vietnam jungle,
In the deadhead of night,
There's a US Marine,
And he's lookin' for a fight.
So don't cry for him, honey,
Don't you shed him any tears,
He's a US Marine,
And he's lived throughout the years.

Bags shook it off. Many who fight in wars have no bone for romance. Many, and among them some of the best and most hardened and lethally skilled, skip over the poetry or, at best, think back on it years later when the hair has mostly fallen out and profile pics shout of the glory days. But to others, Bags most certainly being one, they recognized when an aspiring warrior meets one who long ago marched to a now silent drum.

New drums were being beaten, out in the farmlands and on skinny black roads leading to and from that monster Fallujah. Every single day the platoon went out, more and more barriers were being erected by combat engineers. Vast staging areas—"iron mountains"—were being built by support groups. These were filled daily with enough food and ammo and spare parts to resupply a great and violent effort; one where storming street by street, door to door, everyone knew, would soon commence. And those whom fate had tapped to participate, for them there would be no way out.

Bags and Carmichael both watched as a friendly convoy rolled up. One, two, five Humvees, Bags counted. Battalion by the look of them, all with their machine guns and grenade launchers manned by turret gunners he recognized from their Headquarters & Support Company.

Out of the lead vehicle stepped the battalion sergeant major. The unit's top enlisted, he was big and broad and wore a constant scowl though he was not known for rash condemnation. A former sniper who'd pulled the trigger in Desert Storm, though his role made some men scurry from his very shadow, Bags had never suffered from him a harsh encounter. The sergeant major walked up to LT and said something. LT nodded and soon called Grass over. Bags watched as Grass's face instantly sunk, his eyes noting the receipt of some ill-gotten news; one that had pulled an entire convoy from elsewhere to come deliver.

Bags left Carmichael and edged closer.

"Do I need to leave right this second?" Grass was asking the sergeant major, looking at LT and then at a string of unchecked vehicles.

The sergeant major nodded yes. "He wants to talk to you."

"I'm sorry, Pendergrass," LT said.

"Aye, sir," Grass blew out his breath. "Me too." The look on his face was as if his boots were in Iraq but his mind was drifting someplace ever further away. And with that, Grass followed the sergeant major to an empty seat in the sergeant major's Humvee. From behind that inch-thick, ballistic glass,

Grass peered out at his team. They had clustered, all standing with question marks.

Grass had said nothing, nor did LT when Bags asked what the heck was going on. The lieutenant only said it was a personal matter.

They resumed their VCP, another man light, looking for guns and bombs that may escape the coming fury.

The leaflets had all been dropped. Word was that no one was allowed to leave Fallujah now.

Back in camp, orders had been given. Certain units were to pack their gear. Not just flak jackets and ammunition, but any and all personal items. These units, to a man, were to be the ones serving as tip of the spear. Those with a morbid bent suggested this was the higher-ups' way of expediting the mailing stateside of belongings from the soon-to-be dead, and even those less inclined to cynicism spoke furtively of how much sense this made.

And then a second order came in: no running off to the internet center to fire a quick email to Mom. No one was to leak what was happening. Trailers were being emptied. Motor pools were being emptied, too; trucks lined up on the hardball just outside the wire. Kickoff was days away, and Battalion had been tasked with looking out for reinforcements.

Bags and the rest of the platoon were receiving such orders

still. Yesterday, Grass had been pulled out of the field without explanation. Bags's watch read 08:01, and LT had them around the hood of his Humvee.

Since the coalition effort had long been to isolate the enemy from the rest of the civilian population, Fallujah had to stay sealed. Eyes were on all exits. Any last-minute stragglers were now to be turned around and ushered back toward the city. Enough time had been given. Enemies were about. Worry had come down that a sizable force was still in the farmlands; anywhere from the houses a grenade's toss away to south of the Euphrates. It was this latter group that LT had been tasked with, and now he divided his teams.

Bags was last to get assigned a dot on the map. Each of the four team leaders was given their own observation post; a strategic lookout on the north shore of the Euphrates. Concerns were high that, once the fighting in the city commenced, enemy reinforcements were going to ford the river and undermine coalition efforts with a bath of blood. Observation posts, or OPs, were the Battalion's learned contribution to prevent that.

OPs had been around forever. Whether temporary or fixed, their intent was simple: to watch for enemy movement. Recon was especially apt for the task, and laden with binoculars and extra batteries for Murray's radio, Bags and the remnants of his team stepped off.

Insertion into an OP was supposed to be done under the cover of darkness. It was what their forefathers had done in the jungles of Vietnam. It was what an entire generation of long-dead warriors had done in the trench warfare of the Somme. Traversing open spaces in broad daylight was suicide, or at least a surefire way to give up one's position. Not much use sneaking into a quiet nook to observe the comings and goings of an enemy if the entire enemy host was let on to your whereabouts.

But orders were orders, and what LT had been commanded had come down with much haste. Beyond adapting to the needs of generals, by marching to the river for all to see, Bags, Jim, and Murray, with Carmichael in tow, could fulfill an ongoing demand of the war effort: presence patrols.

These patrols were the thorn in the side of all who wore the uniform and proudly carried the gun. It was a strange thing to want to fight but not to kill. Bags had long considered what events may have led up to a young man from the Middle East abandoning whatever life he had to pick up an AK-47 and fight the Americans. Maybe it was a sense of duty. Or a sense of protecting what he knew and held dear. Maybe those whom he respected pointed that young man in the direction toward war and said "That way your destiny lies." And if so, that young man listened. Many of them did. And if so, Bags could hardly find a difference in his enemies than his brothers who now walked with him toward a riverside OP.

But killing was as necessary to armed conflict as was conflict itself. The heart hardened, and the mind shimmered a shade different; wishing from a place deep inside the desire to put a hostile man in one's sights and then pull the trigger.

Presence patrols were the opposite. To walk up and down, all over Iraq, yelling in everyone's eye "The Americans are *still* here!" This was not combat operations. This was a slogging tactic that sprouted as a reaction to mitigate booms in the insurgency.

Presence patrols came with all sorts of humanitarian attachments. Sometimes warfighters passed out candy, or cigarettes, or did knock-and-talks where interpreters stood next to LT and asked farmers "Where are the terrorists?"

And now the team, without Grass, was on another, a presence patrol, defiling the covert nature of recon. But at least they had a journalist with them—he had to be good at hearts and minds.

"Mr. Carmichael," Jim said as they went up to their first berm. "You dealt with Iraqis much?"

"Quite a bit," he said. "But way more during Desert Storm. Back when you were a pup, Jimmy."

Murray asked, "How was it? I mean, was it anything like this?"

"The few times I went out with the grunts, the Iraqis were all giving up."

"So then definitely not the same," the whole team seemed to say.

"Pardon me for asking," Jim said, "but you got out and jumped right into writing?"

"More or less," said Carmichael. He was walking with his hands in his pockets, like a grandpa strolling in the park. Carmichael looked up to the blue. "Started with newspapers and colleges and everything in between...but I belong out here."

"Sounds like you've been just about everywhere," Murray said. "Home life get boring?"

Bags listened as Carmichael laughed and said something about where he rests his head is home. There was more; Jim, for one, had something close to fallen in love. Later, he would say it was the old man's kindness. That someone had fought in multiple wars and was still tromping around with men a third his age was commendable, and what was even more was that no amount of years in the deserts and jungles and the freezing cold had robbed him of his cheer.

Jim and Murray questioned Carmichael about war and life and if he saw tigers in Nam, and Carmichael was happy to answer them. Now that they'd been "in country" almost two months, Bags felt something like being at home. As they traversed a planted field, he knew which color of Iraqi earth would be dry, which would mean packed down hard, and which held just under its surface a wet, slippery, sometimes surprisingly deep clay that could trap in place entire Humvees. Reaching the other southern edge of a field, they entered a thicket of palm, and not a sparse flower was unfamiliar to him. Nor were the trees themselves or the blades of grass beneath their boots. But home Iraq was not, for the young man found himself drifting away; thinking about women. Not as in the barracks, where noisy smut played endlessly from computers, he thought about women and how much he wanted one, needed one, one day, and how such distractions, he reminded himself, were presently so very dangerous. From behind him, Jim and Murray and Carmichael's boots crunched down on fallen palms.

Bags pulled himself from his soul-searching and back to the march toward the river. Now through the trees, he could see up ahead there was another berm, and on it a road. He remembered from LT's map this was the last hardball before their final stretch. Once they were up and over, it would be two kilometers straight south until they met the water. As they approached the berm, it became clear the earth elevating the road was made of fertile soil; tall grass growing all the way up its side.

It was only when they were up on the road that they saw it. Close enough to be hit with a well-flung stone, after another stretch of field there was yet another road; yet this one was made of dirt and resting on no berm. It was level with the earth and its sides were as soft and bare as the road itself. And on the side nearest, Iraqi men were busy digging a hole. There were three men, all of them with their backs to the Marines.

"Down!" Bags quickly whispered, knowing *that* wouldn't last long. Soon, those men would turn. Everyone, even Carmichael, took a knee and hid amongst the high grass, having instantly sidled down the berm until only their heads poked over the road. Sure and certain, one and then two of the men began to look around; their eyes passing right over the team. The third man continued with his shovel.

Bags didn't need to see, he knew. He sensed Murray reach for his handset and open his mouth but then say nothing. What was there to actually report? They knew what it looked like— what it most likely was. Bags squinted. He searched, though the eye-level grass and the disrupted earth at the men's feet made for many obstacles. No IED could be seen. If one were holding an artillery shell, there would be gunfire first and reporting after. But until some blatant and hostile act could be clearly observed, Bags and his men would stay quiet on a knee.

Funny, but Bags wished right then that he could consult Carmichael. A part of him thought the former platoon sergeant would, at any moment, issue an order that they'd all happily follow. Bags, too. But the old man said nothing; no one did, and they waited.

"How long does it take to dig a darn hole?" Jim soon whispered at Bags's elbow. Their mission was to set up an observation post, and before getting there they'd found themselves doing exactly that. Bags heard Murray tapping his watch. A comm window was coming. They'd need to report this, but just one word uttered too loud would give them away. And then what? Dirt was still flying, but they needed to move.

Bags turned and nodded to Jim, and whispered to everyone, "Y'all see how our road here curves toward theirs a bit?" Bags pointed out to his left, eastward, to where the berm they were all kneeling on indeed pushed a little closer to the Iraqis. "Let's go."

Murray took point, ducking low and moving off the berm. He picked up his pace and Jim followed. Behind them, Bags stuck the buttstock of his M4 into the pocket of his shoulder and entered a light jog.

They spilled out on top of the road and now it was in motion. "Halt!" Bags yelled to the Iraqis. There was no stopping Murray from charging; rifle pointed at the Iraqis like a toy soldier gifted with sudden flight.

Two were gone so fast it was as if they hopped in the hole they'd dug and simply vanished. The other, though, the Iraqi who'd stooped down to retrieve something, looked at them with big, wide, white eyes; a shadow of terror across his face. He dropped what he was holding. He stumbled backward, he turned, he began to flee, but Murray tackled him down.

The tackle was overdone.

Murray flattened him with such force that he rolled right over the Iraqi, who kicked and squealed and shot to his feet like a spring. Murray, tied up in his rifle's sling, gorilla'd the rifle behind him, crouching with his hands out in front as the two now eyed each other.

Unbelievably, the Iraqi went for his legs. The man was small and in a solid black "man dress", making it appear at times as if Murray was wrestling with a wild dog. The Iraqi pounded with his fists and he shrieked in Arabic, all the while Murray used his weight to pin him to the earth.

Marred by dirt and grime, helmet cock-eyed, Murray swung his eyes over. "Little help here?!"

Oh, right, Bags thought, snapping out of it. He ran over. "Get in there," he growled, grabbing one hand by the wrist, working one loop of his flex cuff over the Iraqi's hand then cinching it down.

"Jesus!" Murray cried. The second hand was much harder, and their detainee squirmed with all his might.

"Jim," Bags grunted, prying the man's fingers from his throat, "You be keepin' an eye out for his buddies."

"Aye, Corporal."

Bags had never heard Jim be so formal with him, but with the adrenaline dump he figured his second man was being serious. "Gotcha!" Bags leered at their prisoner, who was now cuffed with both hands behind his back. "Lift him up, Murr'."

"With pleasure," Murray said, hoisting the man skyward by the flex cuffs so that he cried out in pain. Their detainee was on his tippy-toes, having been lifted right out of his sandals. "What the hell'd you fight me for?" Murray growled in his face. "Huh? *Huh?*" Murray held the flex cuffs higher, forcing the man to bend down and his shoulders scream.

"You boys better come take a look at this." Carmichael was standing near the hole; near where their prisoner had dropped his: "IED."

"I knew it," said Murray, who if it weren't for the presence of a journalist may have belted the Iraqi in the ribs.

Jim wanted nothing to do with it. Murray put the man on his knees and scanned the horizon. Bags moved over to Carmichael.

Lying on the ground was an old Russian mortar. It was an industrial gray. The tail fins and body clung to a soil different in color than the earth at their feet. *They dug this up from somewhere else*, Bags thought, staring at the wires running out from where its fuse head should have been.

"This was going to get connected to a cell phone," he said to Carmichael.

"Indeed. A phone one of those other two must've run off with."

"Murr'!" Bags yelled. "Check and see if he's got a phone."

"Already checked him," Murray said. "He's got nothing. Not even a wallet."

Bags surveyed the area. The Iraqi's accomplices were gone, and if not gone they were hiding well enough. "Jim," Bags said, "you relieve Murray. Murray, call this in. Tell LT we'll need EOD to blow a rigged mortar, and," he said rather proudly, "we got him a detainee." He turned next to Carmichael, who was smiling. "Anything else you think I should add?"

"Nope," Carmichael said. "Well done."

The deed was called in. Murray reported to LT all that had transpired and soon four Americans and one Iraqi were seeking the refuge of a palm tree's shade.

"We're going to wait here," Bags told Jim. "Man, LT sounds excited." And he most certainly had. This was their first official detainee. That two had escaped only hammered home all the harder why their unruly captive would need to be questioned by specialists back at Camp Fallujah. Accolades and maybe a medal were forthcoming.

Carmichael popped their bubble.

"You have to wonder," the old man said, "if those Alzilal are watching us right now. Oh, don't look so surprised, I have heard of them too. Every reporter from here to Tikrit is aware of a group plaguing the battle space."

"Does it make you wish you had a gun?" Bags asked. "We could probably pull you something out of a cache."

But Carmichael only said, "Some say they're Syrian. Others, mercenaries from the Caucasus."

Bags felt the cool black metal of his rifle. "Who do you think they are?"

"I do not know, but whoever they are they're most dangerous."

"...So they're just going to roll up, all on their own?" asked Jim: *They* meaning LT, his comm guy, and the platoon corpsman.

"Sounds like it," said Bags. "Our OP will have to wait."

"Not like we should do one now anyways," Murray said, heeding Carmichael's words and rising to his feet while everyone else, including their Iraqi, still sat in the grass. "Those two have probably gone and alerted everyone." He looked up at the pitiless sun, the exposure it cost them. "We'll be walking into a death trap if we head to the river now."

And there they waited, seemingly forever, as Murray's sun crept closer to noon.

The heat increased as the day went on. Looking the direction LT's Humvee should have been coming from, they saw nothing but the elevated road they'd all hurried over. No wind blew and the Marines sucked down water and fiddled with their weapons while Carmichael wrote in his notepad.

Carmichael soon asked them about themselves. He asked them about their families, their lives; and they were eager to answer. Bags commented on the fact that Carmichael was writing without end, and the older reporter smiled and said that he may put it all in a book one day.

It was a strange thing, how facts and memories once jammed in one's skull slowly leaked out. In boot camp, Bags had learned much of Marine Corps lore: Hue City, Chesty's five Navy Crosses, Lieutenant Presley O'Bannon and the Mameluke sword. But as the sun stared at them from on high, Carmichael began to tell them stories of his own, and based on many questions Jim and Murray had first asked. Bags recognized some of them, but many of the tales he did not, and he began to wonder if these had been beaten into his head in boot camp and he'd simply just forgotten. Bags and his team knew about skateboarding, and prank calls, and movies about the redemptive power of violence. Carmichael knew Marine Corps history, history in general, of an America now-gone, of battle sites not taught in books, of warriors young and old, but mostly young, dreadfully young, who reached the stars with the heroism that took their lives. They wondered how many books he'd read, and if he'd, too, once wanted to die in battle.

"Since all teams are at their OPs," Murray said.

"All of them but us," Jim interrupted, making a show of them sitting.

Murray continued, "There's no spare team. So, if things go

south it'll be up to LT and the comm guy to come play savior."

LT definitely needed to show up. It wasn't that far. What was keeping them? Bags took his mind off the temptation to brood and turned to Carmichael. "Do you have any valiant comm guy stories?"

"Indeed," he answered. "And I have you one better. I trust all the running and gunning and jumping out of perfectly good airplanes hasn't rattled loose your knowing of Belleau Wood."

"Not yet."

Belleau Wood, the famous WWI battle site, was where the US Marines in many ways were born. Sure, they'd marched and shot and fought and won in Haiti and Nicaragua and the shores of Tripoli, but there, in BW, their modern mystique marched out of the murky forests of France with its head held high.

Carmichael nodded and grabbed his water bottle. He held their detainee's chin and helped the man drink. As he did, he said, "During Belleau, a wounded Marine took the shards of a bayonet and with it he charged forth to fight the Germans. What was more, he'd been some type of clerk, one who was in the wrong place and at the wrong time...or at the right time, for he took three with him."

There was a silence, and then there was finally a rumble; a mechanical growl coming up from the other side of the berm. Jim saw the turret of the Humvee first, and he waved and announced that the platoon corpsman was manning the machine gun.

"There they are," Murray said, hoisting their detainee onto his feet.

"Sorry we're late," LT said, "but we had a surprise delivery." Out from the back of the lone Humvee emerged Grass, in full gear, smiling and waving as if he'd been gone a full month.

"Grass!" cried Murray. "We thought you up and left us, halfway to home now because you can't take the heat."

"Not on your life!" said Grass, coming up and giving each of them a fist bump. "Good to be back. The team's back up." And it was, and as Carmichael began to tell the lieutenant how well his men had acted, the four stood under the sun; good and whole. It was immediate, however, that something was still wrong. Though Grass forced a grin across his freshly shaven face, the grin looked plastic and his skin looked pale.

Attention was turned to their Iraqi. LT asked for the run down again and Bags gave it, escorting him over to the hole and to where the IED lay. EOD was summoned and given coordinates over the radio and they said they were on their way. LT took hold of the detainee, checked his flex cuffs, and then guided him to a rear seat in the Humvee where the comm guy blindfolded him.

Grass clung to every word. Smart was the decision of Bags. Glorious and hilarious was the fumbled tackle of Murray. He'd wished he'd been there, he said—here, where he would have beaten them all to the punch and either speared their guy better or run off to catch the other two. But yet in all this talk, it was all the more clear something was eating him.

Bags was the first to ask.

"Yeah," said Murray. "What's going on? Why'd they pull you?"

Grass was holding his SAW but then he let it hang by its sling and then he rested his elbows on its black metal. He sighed, not so much in sadness, though sadness was there; more a man who knew he had to speak of something in which he didn't wish to.

But he did: "My brother," he said. "He's dead. Killed himself. Battalion offered me a plane back to the States for the funeral."

"My god, Grass," Bags said.

"Yeah, I would have had to sit out the rest of the deployment." Grass sniffed. "The colonel sat me down and asked if I wanted to go home."

Murray put a hand on Grass's shoulder. "We're sorry to hear this, man."

"I told the colonel no."

Bags, Murray, and Jim all looked at one another. Family back home may be ill-started seeds in spoiled soil, but here, young and armed and at war, these men were alive.

Grass made a despairing noise. "My brother had problems

for years," he said. "And I'm never going to see him again."

Bags couldn't help but stand there and imagine what Grass's brother may or may not have looked like. He pictured someone a lot like Grass; but one riddled by drugs and failed jobs and withering, dying, gone. Bags stared down at what little vegetation grew under their boots. It was going brown and soon would be dead and he couldn't shake the thought that this was just the way of things.

But Grass hadn't left his teammates. Even the wild idea that he would had shown that their colonel didn't truly know his men…or maybe the old colonel did, and he'd known presenting the option to Grass was a formality but knew his operators, to a man, would turn such things down.

"Hey," Murray then said, "didn't you put up over three hundred the other day? First time ever?"

"Yeah," said Jim, going with Murray's brightened tone, and he reached up and grabbed Grass by his face. "And you may not see your brother again, but you will still see this ugly mug, ha!"

Color came back to Grass's cheeks.

"You've got a good team here," Carmichael said to Grass, who'd overhead much and now stood behind him. "It's been a short period, but I'd say I've gotten to know them well enough." The old man took him by the shoulder and led him out of the ring his team had formed. Grass walked alongside him, as if the two had known one another for years. Bags could not see what Carmichael said, only that he was talking. Grass listened and sometimes nodded, loud enough saying "Thank you," so that Bags could hear.

Bags watched them as they looked out at the horizon.

Then there was a sudden appearance of Humvees.

"Boggs," the lieutenant said as Bags counted three. "Go show EOD where that mortar is."

"Aye, sir," Bags said, joined by Murray and Jim. Out of one vehicle stepped the EOD guys, now familiar faces; portly Marines who both wore proud mustaches. Guarding them were the other two Humvees; open backs filled to the brim with armed, staring grunts.

"Will ya look at them," Jim whispered. Indeed, up in those bare and exposed Humvees scowled down the hardest type of warfighter; dirt-laced body armor with clean weapons, hard as coffin nails with scowls to match. Bags nodded and they continued on, soon showing the explosive experts where their next duty waited.

When a fire team of grunts jumped down to provide EOD's security, Bags walked back to Grass and Carmichael. He had figured he'd hear a conversation about life and death and acceptance. Certainly, the two were still staring that intensely out at the lands to the east. But as Bags neared he heard Carmichael saying, "You don't see it? Right over there." They were talking now of something very different.

Bags followed where Carmichael now pointed. Grass must've seen nothing, too, for he said, "No, I don't. By the way, what's the name of the mag you write for?"

"It's called *Dignity*," Carmichael said dismissively. "Okay —look now. Under that cluster of trees. You don't see that man kneeling?" Carmichael had one hand shielding the sun from his eyes. The other was still pointing: "Over there. And it looks like he's got a phone."

Then, as if conjured by the word, Bags and Grass saw a

bright shimmer. It was gone before it had fully appeared, but now they saw indeed a man in all black, crouching under the shade of a tree.

"What was *that*?" Jim asked right behind them, nearly scaring Bags out of his skin.

"You see that guy hunkering down over there?" Bags asked back.

"I don't, but what's *that*?" Jim was pointing in a different location now, though not far from what was surely a man trying to avoid being seen. Jim got flustered and tried to direct them to where he was looking, saying he wasn't sure what he was looking at, only that it looked like a black speck on the horizon. "Ugh," he groaned. "Now it's gone."

"Thirty seconds," an EOD tech yelled. This, they knew, meant the mortar was hooked up and was now less than half a minute from being destroyed. The EOD guys and their grunts were moving back to their Humvees. Bags and Jim, Carmichael and Grass, all turned and rejoined Murray a bit further away. A moment more and the explosion coughed up a thick cloud. As Bags knew they would, the techs had placed the mortar in the nearby hole and constructed the detonation to blow out and down rather than up and out.

"Still," Murray said. "It's always fun when you feel that blast in your feet."

With the mortar blown to bits and one of its former owners in LT's Humvee, the lieutenant shouted that all vehicles were leaving. They were heading back to Camp Fallujah; one grunt Humvee taking up the rear, EOD and the other grunts in the middle, and LT up front, taking lead. Bags and his team and the old man watched as they rolled off the field in a single file, up onto the road. It was when the third vehicle got on the asphalt that the IED went off.

An explosion tore through the air, much meaner than the previous, and with it came a fountain of dirt. Bags saw for a brief moment a towering flame; a tongue of orange fire that ran up the far side of the EOD vehicle and then was gone. LT's vehicle stopped. The grunts in the turrets shouted, gripping their machine guns, and Bags and his team watched as they called out, looking left, right; for any sign of the enemy. EOD's vehicle limped until it met the Humvee in front of them with a slight crash. They poured out, running around to the side where the blast had happened and were soon meeting LT on the road. Everyone who stood there looked fine. Though rattled, none were without arms or covered in blood; a macabre scene Bags had half-pictured.

The EOD guys looked shocked and happy to be alive. But just as they were, so too was Bags. He could hardly believe it. That IED, what had to be another damned mortar, went off right where he'd had his team take a knee. Under grass that high, that IED was one that had been long buried. If there had been a phone, they had all simply not seen it. That could be forgiven, their eyes had all been on the men digging, but now Bags joined the grunts in their scan of the horizon. This place was a hot spot.

"There he is again!" cried Jim. "That black speck!"

"That's no speck," Bags had pulled out the binoculars and had them now honed in on: "Alzilal—look!" he said, giving the binos not to Jim, but to Carmichael.

The old man gave him a puzzled look, but he took them. He scanned and suddenly stopped. "It appears Jim's speck is a forward observer." He handed it to Jim next, who was eager for a look. "And he's got our phone man with him, Bags."

Jim laughed hoarsely, "Yep, two vile creatures dressed in black. One's lookin' right at us with a set of binos all their own."

"That's their observer," Carmichael said. "The other must've called the IED."

Tyler turned and looked for LT. "Sir!" and he told them what they saw. LT ran over and needed no glass; everyone was pointing. As Murray and Grass took their turns with the binoculars, oathing with increasing intensity the violence they'd commit, the lieutenant packed everyone back in the Humvees. Everyone except Bags's team and their attachment.

A mad scramble began. Murray put an ear to his handset and relayed as best he could that LT was telling EOD to get back to Camp Fallujah but for the grunts to follow him. He was heading for the duo in black, but now EOD apparently said hell no and was on LT's bumper, and so the convoy of four, machine guns locked and loaded, took off: a metal snake, storming up dust as they departed.

Bags grabbed the binoculars. The Humvees went east, up and over berms, near a canal's swift edge, broadsiding into someone's yard to see if they were hiding the dreaded Alzilal; the shadows who continued to pester them. Then the Humvees could be seen no more.

After a time, LT was back on the radio. Along with the grunts, he'd hunted the area but they all were no closer to neutralizing the threat than they were an hour ago. "No joy," he said, and informed them EOD now had possession of the detainee. EOD and the grunts were en route back to Camp

Fallujah and LT was now heading back to the platoon patrol base.

Murray handed Bags the handset. "Carry on with the OP or hump it back here," ordered the lieutenant. "Up to you, team leader."

"You know, I gotta say," Jim adjusted his helmet and scratched his chin. "I think I've seen more wacky tactics in one day than most see in a lifetime."

"Because LT's letting us choose?" asked Bags.

"No! That those Alzilal detonated that bomb when our detainee was in one of our vehicles. Guess they don't care much for those on *their* team." Jim chuckled. "And wackier yet, LT left all our Humvees unattended to come out here. Guess there wasn't much choice, though."

"And speaking of choices," Carmichael said, "you now have a choice. What's it going to be Bags? Do we head back?"

It was a good question, one that had his whole team watching him. Not knowing was a sure sign of a weak leader, even in a team as democratic as theirs. Still, there were things he needed to consider. Much had to be weighed. The truth was they'd kicked up such a mess even the remotest level of secrecy was pure fantasy. There were two IED planters who'd run off, two Alzilal who'd watched the Marines like hawks, *two* explosions in almost as many minutes, and then there was that wild goose chase that ended up turning up nothing. And yet, these same events held promise of their own. Their stalkers had been pushed to hiding, and if they were looking for anyone now it would hopefully be a wild string of approaching Humvees.

Bags said, "I do not think we will be watched anymore today." He saw all his men's eyes brighten. "And the river isn't far. Call it in, Murr'. Grass, lead the way."

Everyone called Pendergrass "Grass" because in the military brevity was the norm. But also because he was wild and unbridled. He boasted a lack of impulse control that could land some in the brig. When he and Bags were seen together just the two of them, "Bag of Grass" became their moniker for some of the senior enlisted; chiding a rather subdued team leader and his party animal subordinate. Grass had said he'd smoked weed by the half-ounce as a teen, but he'd given it up. Not just because piss tests and Parris Island were coming, but it knocked him from first place to third in a sprint triathlon he'd sweat and bled for since he'd turned fifteen.

Grass had passed ARS with flying colors. He'd also almost gotten booted twice. The first was for an empty whiskey bottle that an instructor found in his wall locker. The second time had to do with an incident out in town; a scuff-up with locals where the police had been called. Bags hadn't been there, but Murray had, and Murr'd said if it weren't for Grass's charisma and run times he would have been let go. Grass came to Battalion a liability, and Gunny Ulfe told Bags that guys like him could be a team leader's worst nightmare, or their greatest asset.

After they'd returned from Iraq, Jim was soon attending Sergeants School. Murray had been selected for combat dive and was busy getting sharked in the Area 5 Pool from sun up to sun down. Bags and Pendergrass found themselves attached at the hip.

And so a mighty summer began. They traveled most weekends, sometimes further than they were allowed but they never got caught. There was, of all things, a sprint triathlete's club in Charlotte, one full of college girls and guys who had sponsors. Bags would go and watch Grass compete. After the race, most of the athletes would head over to a health food restaurant that also served beer. It was a vast departure from the beer drinking back at the barracks, where since completing a combat deployment, Battalion's now-hardened warriors drank as Vikings returned from the northern shore.

Bags and Grass grew to love that restaurant, and they laughed how only months prior their tofu and ceviche had been cocoa beverage powder and country captain chicken pulled from the confines of a MRE. The folks who raced alongside Grass were curious about their experiences. There was no hiding their haircuts, nor would they if they had been able. They were proud of their service, and slowly the crowd warmed to pose broad, global, political questions to which the Marines mostly laughed and said it was above their pay grade. But there were the occasions where a question was easier to answer; stuff about weapons and how often they got to shoot them and what guns they'd recommend for home defense, or for the "creeps" back on campus. Some of the athletes even insisted on buying them beer, the weird IPAs with the weirder names that usually tasted like chalk, but Grass and Bags were much obliged. As best they could, they talked nothing of their war, or their deeds, hoping to enjoy this odd venue as long as it lasted.

The final weekend of the Charlotte experience, right around the time Jim was completing Sergeants School and Murray was neck-deep in mile-long fins, two new athletes joined the club.

They ended up in an apartment after that weekend's race. There was much music and dancing, and Grass gyrated and boogied with the best. Bags, as had been his standard operating procedure, sat back and soaked it all in. It was fun to watch, more fun to use another moment on the sidelines to slide over and try to talk to a girl.

Both of the new athletes were girls, in fact. And neither wanted to talk to him. They were patently "anti-war," and wore it like a headstall each time the opportunity rose to sneer at him and Grass. The girls would rasp in highborn whispers, "Why are *they* here?" When the guy who lived in the apartment shrugged his shoulders and vanished into the crowd, new and lively thrusts were given. The two Marines probably voted for Bush, probably ate mostly hamburgers, they probably had diesel trucks and were only coming to Charlotte to roofie girls or to go pick bar fights. They'd roughed up innocent children in Iraq—or was it Iran?—and, above all, were definitely not capable of digesting or interpreting the full meaning of songs by O.A.R, Ani DiFranco, and Jack Johnson who sang and strummed over the speakers as the triathletes mingled.

But give it up for an iPod on shuffle and too many beers, for right then the Village People came on and the place came alive. Three guys and one constantly giggling girl, all still in sweat-stained tank tops and neon running shorts, anointed themselves the Y and the MCA and took over where the kitchen met the living room floor. It helped they were all drunk. Bags hoped for their sake it was enhanced by race dehydration, for the Y looked like a wobbly T and the A maintained her giggle as she fell and puked all over one of the anti-war girl's shoes.

The Wobbly T laughed. The owner of the apartment laughed and grabbed a mop. Grass laughed so hard he almost fell over. The girl with vomit oozing down her legs did not laugh, and Bags held his grin in as best he could as he pointed toward the bathroom door.

On any of these weekend excursions, Bags brought his backpack. The military, if nothing else, rubbed off on one's sense of shit could happen. Socks, toothpaste, some loose cash, a spare phone charger: all there. And so were a humble pair of flip-flops, those that when he peeked into the bathroom he offered her. By then her shoes were in the sink and her feet were being scalded by the steaming water coming from the bath. She looked his way for a long moment, then said thanks but no.

Bags could never remember her name, only that she was terribly pretty. She wore her blonde hair in a bun and her top and bottom that day had been the type of pink one imagined California girls wore; roller-skating in the 80s, blowing bubbles of pink gum.

She marched out of the bathroom, joining her friend who

also wore her hair in a bun. The girl who'd puked apologized in the way that drunk people do. Bags understood why the two would be annoyed. He certainly was. Listening to someone slobber sorry over and over made him bristle, as it did the two who feigned their forgiveness and tried to slip away.

The women were then rather short with Bags when he tried to slip in. It was true he sensed an opportunity and was being driven by the forces young men know, but he wasn't being pushy. He asked if they wanted to join him and Grass and go someplace else, someplace where they could be free from the crowded apartment; a drive in his truck where they could hit fifth gear down some open country road. Unbelievably, they accepted, and were soon on the road.

On the drive, the girls berated them. The one who'd been puked on changed plans and demanded the ride was to take her home. Her friend, meanwhile, laughed in Grass's face when he said he'd gone over to help liberate Iraqis. She said liberation was post-facto to going for weapons of mass destruction: a bald-faced lie that was now costing lives. She said most of Iraq was illiterate anyway and that she didn't care what some talking head on a conservative news channel said. Iraq's first official democratic election was a farce. Only a tiny minority of Iraqis who lived in cities—like the city they'd ravaged and now gloated over—were the ones who voted, and who the hell could trust the integrity behind the ballot box? No, their war was stupid; their efforts somewhere between pitiful and psychopathic, and that real men would have just told the recruiter to go fuck himself.

Bags looked into his rearview and told her those who put on the uniform have little say in which way they get directed, only that they, like any other person in any other human convention, could only do the best with what they had. He told her their unit had worked alongside Iraqi soldiers whose family members had been tortured under Hussein's regime, and that those same men, though skeptical of the US's role in the long term, were in no short supply of gratitude. He said, "Oppression is an evil that knows no borders."

She rolled her eyes and told him he needed to grow up: "Grow up, will you? So you trade one oppression for another? You're trying to tell me that those poor people walking around over there—afraid if they look at you wrong they'll get shot—they aren't oppressed?"

Bags told her she made some fair points and that there was no denying the carnage that was still piling. But he also said that intentions, somewhere in this mess, had to matter. He spoke not for Bush, or for the generals, only for himself and the men he'd personally seen act by the guiding rods of courage and integrity. That civilians made the mistake of looking at the military as this cohesive whole, but that it was really many different people with many different points of view. And that they all could have just as well been born in 1925 and the same wind in him had to be in those young men who stormed the beaches of Normandy. That no one chooses the era they are born into, most of all not the military man, and that all that was left was to face death and carnage and despair with as clear a conscience as God would allow. It may sound trite to those who aren't caught by that same wind, but the stated purpose of any war, since Vietnam and especially now, means less to those who fight in it than to those who watch on as spectators.

No more was said. Soon they reached where the girl lived

and both piled out and it was only Bags and Grass in the truck.

There were no more events. Battalion had a new training schedule and those who'd been attending schools were filtering back to the barracks with new murderous skills. Grass had stayed in touch with some of the triathletes on Myspace. One told him those same girls came back a few days later and tried to rail on about the "stupid Marines." It pleased Bags when Grass read to him the full report. The other folks had stuck up for them, saying that if those stupid Marines's behavior was anything like their behavior while overseas, that they couldn't be that bad, and that they seemed like the types of guys who helped someone when they were down.

Some years later, Bags was on a business trip. By then he was out of the Corps and had just started his new job in his new career. This flew him to none other than Grass's hometown.

Ian Pendergrass was now a hot shot realtor—a name and smiling face Tyler saw on at least one billboard shortly after renting his car at the airport. It struck Tyler as odd that Grass would have moved back to where he'd grown up. Grass had that type of "going to LA" aura about him, one of those people who only looked forward, or at least said such things. Nevertheless, the two of them were in the same place for the first time in what felt like ages, and they'd agreed to meet up after Tyler's appointments. Grass promised him, of course, a night he would not soon forget.

That evening, they hugged one another in a parking lot. It was one of those black asphalt parking lots like the roads in Iraq, though where they stood now and laughed at each other's shaven faces was lit by lamps and slicked by a polishing of rain.

They rubbed each other's faces and joked how they'd obviously long chopped off their EAS beards. Grass commented how Tyler looked exactly the same, and Tyler joked Grass's teeth looked so perfectly white that they had to be bought.

And Grass brandished them all night, showing Tyler off to his real-estate buddies. The parking lot they'd met in belonged to a bar; one of those upscale places that once inside doesn't appear so upscale anymore. The place was clean—more than clean. But, *Dear god*, Tyler had thought, *the people*. The place was littered with rich old men and young women, ruthlessly strutting in the highest of heels, from lech to lech. But it was the music that stood out: a forty-dollar cover and the bar was piping in Top 40s on thin-sounding speakers. Not that Tyler minded the stuff, but maybe his mood was soured by the pack of howling realtors who'd gone through their third bag of cocaine and demanded he get up and do karaoke.

All and all, the evening was...okay. Tyler had never known he could wail out Kelly Clarkson, nor had he ever thought how satisfying it would feel to watch a realtor backpedal and apologize in wide-eyed fear when Tyler balled his fists and told the weasel no, he didn't want a snort. It was great to watch Grass in his environment again, though. Be it a barracks party or a gold digger bar, if there were hearts-a-beatin' and people to please, the man was up on a table, beer bottle or microphone in hand, bouncers or some staff sergeant in a duty belt yelling he get his ass down. He always did. And in this case, he then snorted Tyler's apportioned line.

Later, Tyler and Grass broke off and went on a long dark journey through a wet winding alley, popping out the other side to step over needles that all seemed to point toward the moon. A few more streets and Grass took him inside an underground place where a comedian told off-color jokes over the roar of a drunken crowd. After many drinks of their own and several trips by Grass to the men's room, they reentered the night and pushed deeper.

It was a town where "downtown" appeared very much the city. Only a mile out, nothing stood taller than a two-story McDonald's playpen. But where they walked, buildings bulked high and gray against the night. Trees that hung over the street were misted by a feathering of rain. It had poured again while they were inside one of the bars, and what remained caught the orange of the street lights as they walked, making their path a glistening tunnel. Out the other end, soon Tyler saw a cemetery. Its walls looked like their stones and mortar were set and lathed before or because of some great war. But the headstones within were both old and new, and Tyler found after he'd shut the gate that they stood at the foot of Grass's brother's grave.

The cemetery was close enough to that comedy club that Tyler couldn't help but wonder if Grass had planned this. Tyler didn't ask. He put a hand on Grass's shoulder, which Grass shrugged off when he sat down on the wet ground.

Grass said he had more than one family member buried here. He pointed to headstones, some new, some covered in lichen; one was a dim figure where Tyler could not make out dates or a name. Grass said their family had settled the town and that a long-dead ancestor, not buried here, had done battle with the Indians and took an arrow to the heart. Inspired by this, he and his brother had always played Cowboys and Indians as children, often two native warriors, doing their rain dances and hooting.

Grass had to come back because after the Marine Corps, after Recon and Iraq, he found himself a nobody, in LA. Turns out he'd actually moved there, lasting a few months as a struggling actor until his blurry stories of wartime deeds had turned off one too many casting directors. He'd said he'd only went out for the roles having to do "with guns," not because he wanted to but because the acting classes he was taking were filled with MFA grads and surfer busboys who all said the town cast people for what they really are. Are, or were, for Grass was no longer in the military, or a warrior, and he got one callback for a TV show he didn't get before packing up and heading home.

It started to rain again. Grass began to cry. The pain of all the times he could have said or done something to relieve his brother of his awful affliction, to assist him on that long hard way, seemed to pummel Grass now harder than when he'd learned of his death while at war.

To Tyler's surprise, the pain left Grass's face and a smile began to grow; a soft glow across cheeks moistened by weather and tears. Grass didn't have his brother anymore, he did not hear his laughter, nor feel his always-burly hug; yet a forgotten happiness filled Grass to the brim, the feeling he had known when they were together. In times that were better.

Grass shot up and danced around his grave, hooting wildly with knees high as they'd done around backyard campfires. "I am now home!" Grass shouted. "Now, I am home."

The emotion faded, leaving Grass in Tyler's arms, sobbing so uncontrollably not a thing Tyler said was heard. Grass wept and said he'd become an addict and every woman he knew left him and he was going to die alone. He kept his face buried in

Tyler's chest when he asked Tyler to lead him out of this. Tyler spoke softly when he said that he couldn't.

Tyler thought about this the entire flight home. Grass would send him the occasional text message after, bragging about closing on a mansion but never anything about cemeteries or what had happened out in the rain. Tyler dared suggest once that he check himself into rehab, that he'd seen things like this with his sister, but Grass never wrote back. *Home*, that word of all things had stuck in Tyler's side like a twisting bayonet. They were home. They had tightened the drag on the same gear. They'd shot at the same targets; accepting nothing less than dead-center. Now they were back, where the needles clogged the sewers.

Grass was but one casualty. America had become weak and decadent, and so, too, became many of her veterans. It was a struggle, one some say was and is mightier than armed conflict itself, to remain frozen in dignity, rather than thaw out into the miserable myopic puddle of America Now.

America Now: vets standing in their yards on the Fourth of July, pear-shaped, next to signs that say *Please Be Mindful of Your Fireworks*. Those same victims were interestingly absent during the one July 4th barbeque Tyler attended his first year after getting out The local VFW put it on and a morbid curiosity had prompted him. As the fireworks raged outside, the few vets from his generation who'd actually showed up chugged beer and talked about war in all its glory, to later roar in collective mirth and hurl empty cans at the TV when figures on its screen who weren't even vets limped out to sulk and talk about PTSD.

America Now: brand new pickups pulling into old trailer

parks. A sign that said "Irish Pride" but with an Italian flag on it, for some reason sticking in Tyler's mind like a thorn in one's eye. A strange meeting overheard in a stranger bar, one where young revolutionaries bought themselves drink after drink, frothing about their hatred for the rich, later marching past a row of beggars as if the old men had been but ghosts. Children without fathers and men without children, people young and old, but mostly the young, dreadfully young, walking zombified, sometimes into traffic; usually face down in their phones.

Had America so much changed or had a fog simply been lifted from Tyler's eyes? He wrestled over this like he used to wrestle with his Marines only there were no flex cuffs there to help him. He had to weigh the tough wisdom one suffers having returned from war; the sudden crash of fantasy having met reality and the hollow feeling that lingers for a time after. He had to consider perhaps he was just "growing up," and a few years in the Corps had a way of putting an old man in a young man's body. But neighbors had once quarreled, and now neighbors no longer knew one another. And that gap only widened with the passing years, so much that folks who used to break bread were shuffled by a great churn and left with strangers to their left and right with equally poor credit and no one bothered to learn each other's name.

This troubled Tyler, and he found himself longing for a time now passed. A lost and better age.

The men in Tyler's platoon all knew each other's names. As they knew which man hated which MRE, and the ones that he preferred. They knew the first names, their last names, the middle names and even the few people who didn't have one at all, like Jim.

Corporal Tyler Boggs, like all good team leaders, learned his team in ways better than he knew his own family. In Fort Polk, before the war, when the southern summer had unloaded on them heat and rain, in the forests of Louisiana he learned Murray's skin blistered if rubbed against poison ivy and that Grass could fall asleep on a high knee.

After Polk had been the Lejeune training areas, where they kitted up once more and with their heavy rucks broke brush to report on roads and landing zones crawling with grunts. And it was in those patrols that the team became one. What had been more monster than man; one arm longer, one eye pointed sideways, one leg stepping faster or slower than its counterpart; this jangled freak found itself suddenly patrolling as a smooth, able-bodied whole. Bags didn't know when it happened exactly, only they had been patrolling in the Great Sandy Run and suddenly he realized—he knew—Jim would be tiptoeing across that fallen log behind him, and Murray wouldn't care about wet boots and would march right through. And sure as fate, when Bags turned away from the back of Grass's head and looked over his shoulder, Jim was shimmying and Murray stood at the far shore of the little creek, smirking.

It was as if, in the hard hours punished by the wind and rain and burdened by a warrior's gear, he had memorized his men. He now knew if they came upon a linear danger area that Grass would always signal a halt with his hand *before* taking a knee. If they came upon an animal, be it a deer or water moccasin, Grass and Murray wouldn't blink an eye but he and Jim would want to stare. Contact Left or Contact Right, when a recon patrol encounters an enemy on their flanks, real or imaginary, Murray would always dive flat on his stomach.

When the team had to run away was Bags's favorite, for he knew when they broke from their cover to leapfrog like mad, no matter where he put himself, Grass would beat him there. And always he would see Jim, bounding alongside Murray, slightly behind and with a gleam in his eye. These movements Bags came to know like he once knew his father's eyes. In moments of great pride, his dad would crease one and lean toward him, in a sort of "told you so" sort of way. The last time he'd seen this had been when they'd won the Little League championship when he was eleven. He'd been the pitcher and his dad head coach, and upon the final "strike three!"—hats and gloves launched into the air—there he spun and knew it, his father would be leaning forward: I told you so.

Learning one's team so intimately you can predict their faces under cammie paint, spinning to see the happy face of your father, these were—these are the moments you feel as if you are running out the back of your helo, ready for your little yellow cord to do all the work; not stopping until your chute is open.

Bags adjusted in the grass, and he did so without waking. They were in their observation post now, and it was night and it was Bags and Jim's turn to rest. Carmichael was asleep, too. And Bags was dreaming.

He is a boy again, back at the River. The trees somehow are different. Some seem abnormally tall, others are in places where no tree had ever stood. Some look like the baobabs of Africa; their great trunks having no place in a Florida wetland. Whether tall or fat, in place or having come out of a phantasm, at their roots all is rotten. The flesh of the forest, its vines and fallen leaves; stinking up to the heavens as under crawl those that eat carrion.

He finds he is walking barefoot down the old cabin road. The road is the same, cool gray under the canopy and all its little puddles, they ground him: here the path is as it should be. He understands. When he begins to run, he does not stop. Waiting at the end are more trees, but they open up for him like Moses and the Red Sea and suddenly his arms are spread.

The dream ends, for Bags was awoken by arty firing from Camp Fallujah. Bags sat up and listened to the thuds: some Goliath walking the earth again, out in the distance. Jim didn't stir but Carmichael was up, listening. Bags watched Murray and Grass whisper.

"Hell of a barrage," went Murray in the blackness. Their OP was reeds and poles, hidden but for the stars that shined on the river.

"Yeah," Grass looked away from the Euphrates and to his right, which Bags knew was toward the city. It was still out of rifle range, but not out of range of the howitzers. "I bet it's to intimidate the diehards," Grass said, "those hunkered down in Fallujah."

Carmichael shook his head.

Bags thought otherwise, too. Those diehards would take blast after blast, shoot from windows with their last arm and their last eye until at last it was time to pull whatever yellow cord of their own to ignite their suicide. They weren't going anywhere. They were waiting.

Back under the light of day, Bags took a fresh inventory of their observation post.

They had waited until nightfall to make their approach. No good would an OP serve them if they'd inserted in broad daylight, or even under the evening light; that purple-pink that had hung above them as they watched for movement in the field; the last patch of land between them and the Euphrates River.

It was a small field, probably owned by a farmer nearby, green and trim as if freshly tended. They had seen from where they'd hid that whoever owned the plot had erected at its southernmost edge some sort of lean-to that faced the river. The lean-to was taller than a man and slanted at a high angle and from a distance the back had looked like a yellow-green wall, made from the reeds that grew along the river's edge. It struck Bags as very much like a baseball dugout, one where its builder may sit and drink chai, maybe watching the waters rush by.

Now, with Bags's watch saying 14:01, the sun would have been punishing them far worse if it hadn't been for this lean-to. Still, sweat ran down his nose. He put down his binoculars and took a break from scanning the opposing shore. There was much to take in on their own side, too. He had many misgivings about selecting a spot that was *made* rather than found. Something built by another man was rarely in the handbook for clandestine activity. Sure, urban OPs had entire textbooks written on them, but those were positions for well within a city. Perhaps one awaited, once they were deep in the coming hell of Fallujah. For now, though, an absent farmer's construction had to do. They were all aware of their vulnerability, enhanced by the simple fact that whatever vegetation that may have hidden them had mostly been uprooted and sown together: becoming the wall at their backs and the roof over their helmets.

Branches from some tree had been cut and stripped of bark, forming the lean-to's poles and rafters. From these, no man hung weapon nor gear. All body armor and rifles were worn by them or wielded in both hands. Jim was at the far right, on his belly and covering their flank as he'd been doing since daybreak. Carmichael sat next to him. Dead center knelt Bags; M4 slung about him with his eyes going back to his binos.

The map had been correct. From their vantage point they could look left or right, scanning further along the river than at any other point. The Euphrates here was maybe a football field wide; close enough so that house windows on the other side could be seen, and there were many, but far enough to conceal faces of those who may be peering out, AK-47 or RPG just below the sill.

Grass lay to Bags's left. He had taken the first bino duty and rest would technically have been an order, but someone had to peek through the yellow-green wall to ensure no one crept up on their rear.

And at the very left was Murray, on a high knee, guarding the other flank. Murray was peering over, of all things, an old shot-up motorcycle. The bike had served as quite the surprise when they initially made entry. One would expect tractors and bongo trucks to be parked about in the farmlands, but not a motorcycle. The old machine leaned on its kickstand so rusty and beaten that the make and model had been thoroughly obscured. But the bullet holes in it, those were apparent. The fenders, the exhaust pipe, the once-black gas tank; all shot up. In the night they hadn't seen the damage, but whenever Murray mumbled something about being next to someone's target practice the hair on Bags's neck stood up.

The weeds that still grew on the north shore did so tall and fat. So plentiful were they on the downward slope that the waters nearest the team were completely hidden. Only the middle of the river and the far, southern shore could be seen. And Bags looked out at it all. The water there was so incredibly blue. Its current clipped along at great speed, and though no boats or fishermen were on its glassy surface, he could imagine what strange fish may be lurking below.

Behind him, stretching to his left and to his right, similar fields spanned east and west; broken and bordered by berms and the occasional stretch of dirt road. But here in front of him were the waters written about in the bible, in so many other ancient texts that still pillared the world.

All was quite mundane, by wartime standards. Murray had just made their comm window and Bags still tasted the MRE he'd eaten before he'd relieved Grass. All was dull, until, from the other side, a canoe entered the water.

There was so much defilade over there. A monstrous bush had taken up the shore opposite them. *A far better hiding spot*, Bags had thought. Some three hundred feet away, its roots started at the water's edge and rioted up all the way to the hardball that was skirting the river. On this road opposite the river, cars came and went; not at the rate of the pre-leaflet days, but after the sun had risen the team had counted twenty. In the late morning, a few of these had parked behind that thick green bush, and more parked sometime around noon.

As sudden as an M4 switching from Safe to Fire, the nose of a wooden canoe had emerged out from that defilade. Three men jumped inside and shoved off, toward the north shore: the shore they guarded: the shore no one was allowed to step foot on.

All three of these men were dressed in white. They wore the Iraqi man-dress, though all came with hoods, and they used those hoods to cover their faces. Two of them paddled and the one in the middle sat, hunched over, sullen and still, with his back to the Marines. The canoe was being pushed by the current, not heading for the OP but to some point inevitably due east. This would be to the Marines' left, and Bags scanned where on their side this troublesome vessel may land.

"You seeing this?" Bags said to everyone. He kept his eye on the canoe, and as he did he heard his guys adjust. Soon, all were gazing at the river.

Since landing in Iraq, what had been sold as a war had

been far closer to cops and robbers, or maybe a massive prison and they the prison guards. There were rules, many of them, and the locals had mostly obeyed. Iraq had been the whiplash polarity of compliant folk or IED diggers. But now they were watching brazen defiance, and at a time when the rule of not crossing the Euphrates may mean the use of lethal force. Bags said, "Call it in, Murray."

Carmichael was up on one knee. As was Grass, who'd already put the foremost paddler in the sights of his SAW. "We gonna blast these guys?" he asked. There was an excitement in his voice that Bags could not pin as fear or thrill.

Bags said nothing. He was busy listening to Murray.

"—Copy. I say again," Murray continued, "one canoe. Crossing the Euphrates. Three men on board." There was a pause, during which Murray's face took on a look that Bags didn't like. "Roger. Copy all," he sighed. "Out."

"What's up?" Bags was still keeping his eye on the canoe, no longer needing the binos.

"LT says Higher wants us to go apprehend them."

"And leave the OP?" Grass said, lowering his weapon.

"Apparently," said Murray. "We're gonna be about as hidden as a three-ring circus."

Bags's ruck had long leaned against a pole. There was no point in wearing full kit if monitoring a river for days on end. He looked back at his ruck. "Okay, Murr," he said, putting the binos inside his topmost flap. "You're with me."

The plan was simple, though not clandestine in the slightest. They were to uproot from their position and run along the river's edge, meeting the men as they came ashore. From there, the flex cuffs they'd packed would be put to good use.

Bags pulled three sets from his ruck and stuffed them all in his cargo pocket. "You ready?"

And with that Murray nodded.

Then Carmichael said it, soft and clear, "Will you look at that."

"There's another one!" Jim gasped.

Everyone in the OP saw a second canoe enter the water. Out of the same bushes it had sprung, but much faster this time. Three men again were dressed in all white. Bags cursed himself for having just put away his binoculars, for he wanted to try and make out the front paddler's face. Whoever he was, like the two men behind him, he trudged forth across the blue water with his head hunkered low.

"These are heading right for us," Jim said.

And they were. The second canoe had entered the river from the monstrous patch of green further west, and now the current was angling them toward the OP.

Bags felt his hands go cold. "They know we are here." Bags squeezed those same bloodless hands around the grip and handguards of his rifle. "Shit!" he said. "Jim, you guys deal with this other one."

With that, Murray and Bags ran out from the lean-to, around the shot-up motorbike and into the openness of the day. Right away, yelling erupted. It was in Arabic and coming from the canoes and though it was many voices, they all sounded equally desperate. As if something had gone wrong. But no one was more desperate than Bags and Murray when the gunfire began.

Shots rang out as the first sandal touched shore. The blasts roared in Bags's right ear and kept roaring as he and Murray flung themselves into the shallowest ditch in Iraq. A berm, rising no higher than a foot, ran across the lip of the field; where its foremost edge met the slope of the shore. Behind this small berm, the two Marines laid on their bellies. They pressed themselves flat to the earth. They pulled their rifles out from underneath them as enemy rounds tore the earth apart in front of their faces.

Vwweeeeeeep! The sound of AK rounds—long since passed—lacerated the air.

There Bags lay, Murray to his left, separated by an arm's reach. Grass and Jim and Carmichael were still in the lean-to, and gunfire now poured out as if awoken by thunder.

When Bags dared pop his head up to frantically return fire, for a brief but horrid moment he did not pull his trigger. He gaped, for he could still see the men in the canoes. They had shed their thobes as a white eye shutting, instantly opening to reveal its hateful, staring black. The Alzilal were upon them. Now a third canoe was menacing its way across the river, its black-robed man at the helm, cruelly tall, shouldering the AK-47 that put rounds into the lean-to.

The dreaded Alzilal had left their mortars in favor of rifles. All fired AKs. The three men in the first canoe had slipped from his sight, but Murray soon screamed, "They're shooting at us!"

His scream was so high-pitched that Bags barely recognized his voice. "From over there!" Murray had in that time slithered to a better angle, and pointed to the direction of their flanking enemy with magazine after magazine of returned fire. But it was the second canoe that Bags trained his sights on. Right before they were concealed by the brush and slope of the shore, he'd caught the rear paddler's head in his sights and dropped him with a single bullet.

Bags joined Murray's fury as two enemy charged up the shoreline's slope. They ducked just in time to avoid his spray. It took all but his last magazine to keep their heads and weapons down.

The lean-to had not been defenseless. In a momentary lull, Bags heard both weapons from within firing, Jim and Grass calling out to one another, and to him.

"Yes!" Bags shouted. "We're all right." He quickly glanced at Murray. "But we're pinned down!"

"Jim got one!" cried Grass.

Bags began to ask if anyone was hit, but a renewed blast from the bowels of the shoreline drowned his words. The two in front of him were still separated by a stretch of risen land, a stretch so slight a single grenade could make all the difference. From the moment they'd charged, he saw that they wore masks as black as their—*Grenades*! he suddenly thought.

Bags, in an instant, weighed the risk. Even a moment off his rifle afforded the enemy an opportunity. And if they charged, he and Murray would be dead. Still, he groped the grenade pouch clipped to his chest, snapping its one button and pulling out a round green grenade. Murray was shouting that he was almost out of ammo. Bags pulled the pin, and as he did he couldn't help but hope the Alzilal, with all their alleged war mastery, had not mastered English and understood what Murray had just said.

Bags hurled the hand grenade over the lip of the berm, into where he could not see, while Murray blasted the last of his rounds.

The two Marines, pinned and out in the open, burned through their ammo until each bolt in their M4s locked to the rear with a deathly *clunk*. Murray had pinned down the first three, though they had shot ferociously, and in momentary lulls, Murray would scream he'd seen a head or one had slithered closer. Now it was Bags who screamed. "We're out! Jim —Grass, we gotta reload. Our ammo's in there with you!"

"I can't throw it!" Grass yelled from somewhere inside.

Bags ducked as another salvo belched forth. "No," he cried over the fire, "we gotta get *back* to *you*!"

There was no more talking. No plan made, for the plan had long been forged in the training areas of Camp Lejeune. Bags and Murray uprooted themselves and began to run. The sight of them sent the Alzilal into a frenzy; dirt shot up in clumps, grass shot off the dirt, plumes of smoke puffed their momentary violence as one of Bags's bootlaces came undone and were gone. AK-47s were aimed many times, and each time they missed, as Jim and Grass provided cover fire.

Bags and Murray ran around the motorcycle and dove headfirst at their rucks, tearing out the loaded mags and stuffing them in their chest pouches—but not before slamming one in their M4s and sending their bolts home. Their hands were caked in mud. Their eyes, mired with grime and sweat, scanned low to the ground. Their reloads had just gone so seamlessly. As rifles barked and blades of grass were shot in half, a family was reunited. Its four members took their positions.

Jim and Grass laid in a pool of spent shell casings: there was so much brass on the ground that hot casings clung and burned Bags's cheek as he rose. Knocking them away, he knelt next to Murray. Out in that open a bond had been made that was first renewed behind that motorcycle where Murray was already firing. Grass was right behind them—too close—one apt machine gunner could punish them for their lack of dispersion, but they had been choked together by enemy fire, and Grass was going nowhere. Behind him lay Jim and his smoking M4, somewhere in that vague side of their shot-up cover. Carmichael was by his side, one leg draped over Jim's like the machine gunners of old, calling out targets whenever a bedeviled Alzilal dared to try and flank them.

When one tried the gunfight was alive once more. But because Grass had trained himself to swap out SAW drums faster than any SAW gunner in Battalion, his weapon was ever ready. Since Jim's eyes were the keenest, he saw the brief black passing through the reeds. He fired his rifle, getting his second kill. Help was on the way: Murray switched from his radio to his rifle like a man possessed, calling in their fate and then desperately returning fire. Since Murray had prepared for such a moment, his ability to switch from one task to the other was that of lightning.

But for all their skill, still the Alzilal closed in. Those whom Bags and Murray had once pinned had snaked their way ever closer. After a furious exchange, they learned to their horror others had pushed further from the lean-to and now burst from the reeds. AKs were firing. The Alzilal were running toward them—trying to envelop them and get on the backside of their now useless concealment.

If Grass had fanned out bullets to keep heads down and Marines alive, then it was because of this that Jim had earned his kills. Yet one in that final canoe still remained, horridly near. His AK somehow sounded deeper, meaner, like it had a foul spirit of its own, shot from the shoulder of a wicked master. This man, from the reeds, cursed at the Americans in Arabic. Each time they concentrated their fire he'd slip behind some unseen cover, laughing wildly as their ammo depleted.

"Use your grenades!" Bags cried. His was used, but Murray and Grass still had theirs. Grass took the order in a flash. Lowering his SAW and opening his grenade pouch, but when he chucked it into the reeds before them, it went beyond its target and shot skyward a blue-white geyser. And the Alzilal laughed.

Jim was next, rising to a high knee and soon pulling the pin. Their enemy shot at his head, sending him down into his own shell casings; fumbling for the live grenade that had escaped him.

"Oh, n—" he gasped.

"I," Carmichael seized the thing, hurling it into the river, and at the nick of time. "Got it," the old man said, sounding like a whisper as the detonation sent another geyser into the air.

And all the while, five Alzilal battled Murray and Bags. Two seemed to have stalked their way closer. Bags couldn't help but picture the dark reunion of this duo linking up at the water's edge. Maybe they were whispering to one another about what ammo they had left. Maybe they had grenades of their own and were about to pull them. Maybe a billion ways to kill and die—and the other two were still circling to the team's rear, for Murray had shot the third right between the eyes.

"What did LT say?" Grass yelled.

But Murray didn't answer. He and Bags now saw death upon them: they were moments away from being inside an L-shape ambush. The worst place to be on a battlefield, two angles of fire would cut them to shreds. Murray yelped in panic, shrieking, "They're getting behind us, they're gettin' behind!"

Behind Murray and Bags, Grass dropped to his belly. He faced the rear, and now his eyes, though none were able to see, shined with a flame.

"Oh my god!" Murray screamed, for death upon them had taken a new form. He was out of ammo—truly out. There were no more loaded mags in his ruck. Yet this was not what froze his blood. The two Alzilal, they had also run out of bullets. But they'd brandished machetes and, mere feet from the back of the lean-to, the cruel sun was shining on their blades.

Bags still faced the enemies in the reeds, and a sudden explosion behind him made him cry out.

Gunny Ulfe had always said to take at least one claymore.

Claymore mines: the USA's favorite directional, anti-personnel death dealer; detonated by remote-control clackers; shooting a wide spray of metal balls into the front-toward-enemy kill zone.

Never had Gunny Ulfe's wisdom shined the greater, for Grass had set the claymore during his watch of the rear. There was no more back wall, nor were there living enemies outside it. Grass still held the clacker in his hand. "I got 'em," he said, having sent them to ruin.

All was silent. Moments of combat victory were seen only in war movies, not in a farm field in Iraq in late October. What things they could tell Gunny! Bags and Murray looked at one another. Murray, that face growing gold in the sun, smiled from ear to ear. He grabbed his handset and to the lieutenant he said, "Sir, no one is hit. Enemy still in the AO, but no one is hit. Over." Bags heard crackles come from the other end, recognizing their lieutenant's voice. Murray nodded and put down the handset. "He says they're on their way."

"Yeah, no shit," said Grass. "ETA, though, maybe? We still got three in the bush." He pointed his SAW muzzle at the reeds; toward the hidden downward slope of the river.

As if summoned by his words, two Alzilal appeared. They were not in front of the Marines but a slight distance out in the field. They were standing as sudden as shadows, having crawled back away, closer to where Bags had laid in the prone against the earth when the battle began. And now they charged; not with machetes, but with automatic rifles. The bursts were so loud they were almost deafening.

Murray was on the horn, his last and perhaps most important weapon. *Yes sirs* and *No sirs* and all the while Bags and Jim were returning fire, and soon Grass was there to join them. Every Marine squeezed themselves behind the old motorcycle, aiming and firing and seeming to hit nothing but air. Bags could hear Carmichael's voice, this time booming: "The one by the water—down there! Don't forget the one *down there*!"

Jim flung himself to the ground, heeding the old man's words with a blast that direction.

"Changing drums!" cried Grass, and after he did, loading his last, he sighted in on a black chest; rushing forward, rifle firing. Then the other chest. And he slayed them, leaving them twitching in their own blood.

Yet before one died, as he was still falling to the earth, he clutched his rifle and one last time fired. A bullet glanced off Bags's helmet, striking so hard that through the armor it still drew blood. It may have been from the very next round, blasted out of that dark barrel, but a piece of the motorbike got shot off and hit Bags squarely in the chest.

But Bags only knew that he'd been hit. He fell back, clutching his chest and gasping for air. Two hands were around him, old but strong, and they began pulling him away. Bags saw Murray's legs spread wide, hunkering low, grabbing for a grenade he would later say he'd forgotten he even had. Carmichael was opening up Bags's body armor, dressing already in one hand, and when Murray's grenade got thrown it went off and Bags swore he saw every piece of flying metal that came up from the reeds. Carmichael was speaking, though what words Bags could not hear, only that they were soft and clear like a bell.

That evening there was a briefing. Intel reports were flooding in. Men sat around the highest table and discussed what had transpired. Much gunfire had gone off that day, and there'd been no shortage of IEDs. Blood had been spilled in the lands encircling Fallujah. Not all of it the enemy's.

Many who had been hit were deemed combat-ineffective. A C-130 was set aside to be filled with those who had to walk up on crutches, be rolled forward in their wheelchairs, or be carried aboard tied tight on a stretcher; IV bags still hooked.

Two days later, the team was shooting their weapons once more. A clear sky had the sun at full throttle and it looked down on them as they shot from the standing, kneeling, and prone on Camp Fallujah's lone gun range.

Not just the team shot. On most occasions, Battalion would alternate what platoon got range time and what platoon didn't. The berm making the range's back end and the two berms providing its lateral limits made for a small shooting space, and the little stretch of sand shooters positioned themselves on was less than a hundred feet from end to end. But on this day there were awards to be given; hastily written and typed up officially, for Bags and his men. Along with no better witness than Carmichael, they had proved themselves victorious, eliminating an enemy that had outnumbered them two to one.

The battalion commander had somehow managed to squeeze every single Marine onto the range, interval by interval, and on this hot and windless morning they were there first making sure all rifle attachments functioned properly and were filled with fresh batteries. Soon they were to roll back out into the fray; battlesight zeroes confirmed and morale heightened.

The shooting was coming to an end. Murray and Grass had finished early and were somewhere, lost in the mass of onlookers as Bags and a few others shot the last of their rounds. Bags was still having a pig of a time; his shot group off, then his group tight but low—and he knew this meant he was looking *over* his sights. He'd quickly corrected the error, though less quickly was dissolving his suspicion his shooting was poor due to being rattled by the charging threat of death. Jim, Murray, Grass, Carmichael too; they'd all felt that same fear, but he'd been the one who'd gotten hit. The smell of gunpowder filled the air as commands came forth from the range coach, some staff sergeant from another company. Bags smooshed in his earplugs and sighted in once more. Three more bullets and Bags was done: shot group finally good.

He walked away and took off his brand-new helmet. Around his head, the battalion saw a wrapped white bandage. The award ceremony would start any minute and, until then, cool shade was the mission. Bags moved to one of the pavilion tents the camp had set up behind the firing line. Jim was there waiting.

"The dead man walks," chuckled Jim.

"I thought I was a goner, Jim."

"You and me both, and Mr. Carmichael too. You should have seen his face when we got your gear off and didn't see blood."

"I've fallen off half pipes," Bags said. "Got hit by punches that felt like sledgehammers. Nothing's ever made me pass out, though."

"It was that knock to the head that KO'd you, surely."

"No," Bags squinted at those still on the firing line; the very tail end of the shooting. "I thought I'd been shot in the heart. I think it was just plain old fear, not my little head wound."

"Little wound nothing. Another inch and we wouldn't be standing here—at least you wouldn't."

"A freaking gas cap," Bags could only laugh, pulling from his cargo pocket the great souvenir of their gunfight. The bullet had actually knocked off much of its rust, and where the bullet had struck its now shining edge there was a piece missing.

"Reminds me a little of Pac-Man," Jim said, staring at the thing before Bags put it away.

"Reminds me of deat—"

"How long you gotta wear that head wrap, Corporal Boggs?" a familiar voice said from behind them.

"Look whose here!" Jim cried. Bags turned and there was Gunny Ulfe. Gone due to an inglorious gut bug, missions and patrols without him, confronting the Alzilal on the shore of the Euphrates and now here was Gunny Ulfe, back, with his back to the firing line, his face shining in the noonday sun.

"Gunny!" Bags said, remembering his bearing then fingering his bandage. In a much calmer tone, he said, "Ah, a few more days. You're back?"

"I am," the platoon sergeant said. "Shat my brains out until I looked like a runway model." Bags looked him up and down.

He noticed how indeed Gunny had lost some serious weight. "But do you hard chargers even need me around now? You're about to have more chest candy than most gunnys."

"Hell yes, we need you," blurted Jim.

"Yeah, Gunny," Bags fondled the gas cap in his pocket. "It's just, I don't know, different out there without you."

"You boys did all right, from the sound of things. But I'm back, as you say. Ready to get back out there, too. There is much to discuss. Most of it will be said during the formation. And, I must say, you weren't entirely alone." At this Gunny's tone became fatherly, rare among battle-hardened gunnery sergeants, rarer still when talking to those whom they usually barked down at. "LT wasn't far," he said, "and I heard our buddy Carmichael was there; in the shit with you."

"He was," Bags said, seeing then in his mind all the old man had done along the river; before the world went dark, before LT's Humvee came screaming in along with a brother team who'd returned early and rained hell on the other side of the river until Carmichael himself had apparently yelled *cease fire*. "He's really something."

"I know." Gunny looked at Bags and Jim squarely. "He led platoons in Vietnam. We were outside Kabul once when rockets came in. The man hardly flinched." Gunny started to laugh; so hard he had to cough, and he beat his chest, which was still very large and still very much like a barrel. "You got nineteen-year-old grunts ducking for cover and an old reporter standing there like a statue. Unafraid, he was. He—"

"Formation!" a random voice yelled.

"Right," said Gunny. "Let's fall in."

The battalion commander and his right-hand man, the

battalion sergeant major, stood facing the range as the entire unit squeezed in. Soon the battalion formed columns and rows, facing their top two men. The battalion stood; designated by company, then platoon, then down to individual teams. But one team had been told by the sergeant major to stand in a four-man line before the lieutenant colonel.

Corporal Boggs, Corporal James, Corporal Murray, and Corporal Pendergrass faced the battalion commander; their fists balled, arms at their sides; in the position of attention as the lieutenant colonel began to read.

Citations were read. Medals were bestowed. To all four went Commendation Medals, all with golden Vs—the combat device—given for valorous action while directly under fire. Bags's Purple Heart came next, and finally a Bronze Star with Combat V for Grass; who later grinned like an embarrassed child when the battalion descended upon him to rub his head and praise his slaying of four Alzilal.

But first, before such congratulations and merriment, they fell back into formation, for the battalion commander had much to tell. The Battle of Fallujah was days away. They could feel it in their bones, taste it in the air. Entire units had already left camp; positioning their trucks and weaponry god knew where: at the eastern and northern edges of the city, most still inside the wire suspected. As the lieutenant colonel cleared his throat, every man before him bent an ear.

"Men," he began, "what we just witnessed was four of you being recognized, recognized for closing in with and eliminating the enemy. Soon, many of you will be given that same opportunity. The sergeant major and I know you have trained hard, that many of you, only a few years ago, joined the Marine

Corps for this very moment; to do as your forefathers did and go to war. Well, it is here. At our doorstep. It is at the toe of our boot, and in days to come those who've yet to do as Corporal Boggs and his team have done will soon see the power of your training. Now, I have no doubt, nor does the sergeant major, that you will perform your duties to the fullest. One of the great honors of leading a pack of men such as you is to unleash upon the battle space those who were made for it. All I ask is that when you see Fallujah, no longer on a map or far in the distance, but with your own two eyes and it approaching fast, that you remember that this is *your* Hue City, your moment, which all shall remember."

Bags felt that, though no man stirred, an energy flowed through the ranks. The battalion commander was done speaking, and through his sunglasses he looked upon his men in their silence. The sergeant major took the floor.

"Marines," the giant said. "This'll be the last time we're together before we roll out. I want your trailers so clean they're shining like a diamond in a goat's ass. We're rolling into that goddamn city. We won't be clumped together. Some of you will be closer than others, remember. Plans are still in the works, gettin' figured out by men smarter than you or me. The furthest our battalion will be from Fallujah though is Benchmark 42; a hill to the south where we'll be set up for command and resupply."

Bags saw out of the corner of his eye how Murray now leaned toward Grass. "I'd hate to be the sorry sack that gets stuck out *there*," Murray whispered. "Miss out on everything."

The sergeant major swung his eyes at the team. The sudden attention given was not because Murray had spoken, though Murray perfected his impersonation of a statue and stood hilariously still, mouth shut. "The corpses of the Alzilal," the sergeant major went on, "we gained much intel from them."

And indeed they had. Jim had told Bags how LT had rolled up and soon had followed most of the battalion. They swarmed the place like hornets; looking for new enemies and strapping the bodies of the old ones onto the hoods of Humvees. Even while Bags was being bandaged inside the battalion aid station, word was trickling down that the corpses were already providing info as if alive and spilling their guts. From the fabric of their black clothing, to the type of blood extracted off it, the sandals they wore to the curve of the bridge of their noses that would never smell the air again, the dead enemy had been identified, and much had been discovered.

"Much has been discovered," said the sergeant major. "Turns out those so-called shadows weren't so special after all. They're from right here, in this part of Iraq. And though they may have been a bit better than their buddies, they're just another finger on the hand that's become a fist and waiting for us. I'm gonna say that again for those of you in the back: those eight dead Corporal Boggs and his men took out, they represent only a percent of the fighters who wait in Fallujah."

"Eight?" Bags was now confused. "I thought they were *all* dead?" he whispered to Jim.

"No," Jim whispered back.

"You just fainted too fast to see how it all ended," said Grass. Even at a whisper, Bags could hear him snicker.

"Can it, Grass," Jim went. "You just passed out, Bags, before the tall one slipped away."

Murray whispered, "He popped up for just a second."

"Then went back down," said Jim. "Right into the bushes and gone like a snake, he was."

"And no one could find him?" Bags asked softly, as if to himself, and all three whispered back *no*.

This was horrid news. The day's celebration had just been blackened as if by a sudden appearance of rain, and if not rain then the dark cloud that held it before its mammoth burst. One Alzilal was left. The running consensus, too, was he'd been their foul leader. This meant he had probably already slithered back to enemy ranks and most likely was gathering new strength, new arms, new men ready to die. Perhaps these men would be better the next time. Bags knew right then, better than any Marine in formation; they would see that foe again.

Bags stretched a sideways glance until his eyes rested on Gunny. The platoon sergeant seemed disinterested in what the sergeant major was saying, as if he already knew what was being talked of and then some. Gunny Ulfe seemed to be looking past the sergeant major; at Karl Carmichael, who watched the speech from well behind the sergeant major and battalion commander, leaning with arms crossed against a pole that held up a corner of the ammo pavilion. It was impossible to tell from that angle, but it seemed that Gunny was smiling; small and faint.

All this bad and good, stretching Bags like a taught wire, ended when he heard the sergeant major's voice: "The best place for men in a unit such as this," he was saying, "is going to be somewhere where he—where you all—can provide overwatch. Overwatch equals support..."

The words trailed off as Bags thought about what they

implied. Though recon men would rather die than admit it, there may have been a few in the ranks to whom "overwatch" and "support" sounded a welcome alternative to kicking in every booby-trapped door. In a city where mostly grunts would be clearing the houses, support meant helping those grunts, the infantry, and supporting them would likely mean calling in fire missions and taking headshots at what enemy peeked through windows or ran wildly through the streets. And to do so still meant exposure. Support meant combat, still, and as the battalion commander stepped back in front of his men, Bags swore his minor bullet wound felt gaping and large.

"Your sergeant major and I have been advised with the coming operations that we could fan you out across the farmlands. For the duration of the siege, you'd be neutralizing targets that present themselves: those who've squeaked past. And we've been advised that we could have you dig into hides around the edges of the city; taking out any Muj who try to escape. But both these are no-goes, for they are below the acumen of such fighting men as you."

Even in the Marine Corps, there were units run by leaders with no stomach for war. They winced at the off-color running cadence: the one about napalm sticking to kids. They viewed combat success as losing no men, awarding few if any Purple Hearts. To some, war was an obligation of service. Their place was stateside; uniform clean and no bullets overhead. Bags couldn't help but thank his lucky stars that he and his guys had the leaders they did. It was a new problem, one might say, to have those above you romantically assign you to hardship. There was surely such a thing as too much danger. And as Bags listened, the lieutenant colonel's words marched toward that very thing.

"Inside Fallujah," he was saying, "there is something called the Row of Four. These are two-story houses where Muhammed Latif let his forces dissolve and where the insurgency once found its center. It was there, in the Row of Four, where the city's current troubles started, and it is there where some of you may very well go."

"One hell of a place to conduct overwatch," Murray whispered to Grass.

The battalion commander took off his sunglasses, seeming to eye each man in one sweeping pass. "The threat of the Alzilal haunting the farmlands is over," he said. "The war for Fallujah has yet to begin. Your task now is to prepare."

The battalion commander nodded and soon the sergeant major called all to attention. The battalion was dismissed. Grass's praise came and then the swarm faded away. Some went back to their trailers, others the gym, others still walked straight to the motor pool or the supply office; requesting extra ammunition for Fallujah, and maybe an extra spare tire or jack to ensure they got there.

The whole team, along with Gunny Ulfe and Carmichael, gathered under the pavilion at Gunny's behest. Though fall, the sun was burning more like summer, and Gunny told them to take a seat. As they did, Carmichael said, "What's that saying you guys like to use? Two is one: one is none?"

They erupted in laughter when Carmichael pulled from his pocket a shiny new gas cap and handed it to Bags, then quiet settled over them.

"Where'd you get this?" Bags laughed, stuffing the gas cap down his pocket to join the other one. He didn't want it, but he wanted even less to offend the old man's humor.

"Wouldn't you know," Carmichael said, "I saw it lying in the trash. I take it as a good omen for you, Corporal Boggs: your symbol of protection."

"Yeah, and you may very well need it," said Gunny, taking a tone that straightened them. "We all may."

Sitting on the range, under the pavilion just off the firing line, Gunny told them their platoon was getting tasked with "something big."

"Apparently," he said, "your kills on the river have made your team the battalion mascot."

Grass and Murray smiled. Bags and Jim undoubtedly frowned. "It's for this reason that I'm briefing you knuckleheads first," Gunny went on. "LT and I will address the whole platoon later."

"Great," said Jim, "survive near-annihilation to get tossed back in the fire."

"The fire and more," Carmichael said. "But I have some confidence you four will keep me reporting a while longer."

"So you're coming with us then?" Bags asked.

"I am," said the old man. "And I wouldn't have it any other way. You gentlemen would've stacked Koreans like cordwood."

Gunny Ulfe did not hide how pleased he was. These were, after all, *his* men: greenhorns whom he'd trained and placed in their billets based on what his eyes and ears had gathered. And he agreed with Carmichael.

Grass stirred. "Carmichael," he said, "will you be picking up a gun and fighting then? If needs be, of course."

The question wasn't as smart-ass as Bags worried Grass maybe had intended. Poking, was Grass's way of exposing that he was nervous. Four kills and a medal hadn't stopped him from envisioning what hell laid before a team that was now expected to charge headlong into peril. Carmichael only nodded, and he said, "My fighting days are over, young gun." He eyed the team, resting them brightly then on Gunny. "That's for other men now."

Gunny said, "There's going to be multiple insert points. It's trickled down that the one most probable for us is Insert Bravo. Insert Bravo is straight hardball; opening up between two buildings and running straight into the heart of it. Alpha, Charlie, Delta: they're going to other platoons. Some are setting up, shallow in the city. Others will push in deeper. We'll be pushing in deepest, right up and on to the top of that Row of Four."

And there it was again, that term, that landmark sounding way too theatric to have been named by Marines. Bags imagined four tall buildings, something like those painted ladies over in San Francisco, but just barren and mean.

"When we step foot in Fallujah," Gunny Ulfe said, "we'll need to move like a screamin' eagle. Fire will come in and we will return it, and from behind whatever cover we find." Gunny then ended the talk, telling the team they were cut loose to go back for one last hot shower or a session at the gym. "Oh, but then Gunny said, as if having remembered. "Murray, I need you to bring y'all's radios in for a new crypto fill."

Murray had been remarkably quiet. Bags knew that whereas Grass had a tendency to get mouthy and flippant Murray had a mind that ran smooth and cold. He was the strong man, slow to anger, slower to rise, but when he did few men could be more deadly.

A decade after the war, Murray was off the grid. It struck Tyler as funny. Of anyone he'd met while he was still Bags, Murray was the most adept at all things tech. But one day, shortly after the birth of his second son, Tyler received a handwritten letter. It was in his mailbox along with a VA appointment reminder and letters from internet service providers that were still hounding him for his cash. Handwritten, and who the hell did that?

It was from Murray, who gave a brief hello and grid coordinates with a time window when it would be best for "Bags" to come out if he was able.

Tyler consulted the masters of his civilian life; his wife and the work schedule. The in-laws were in route and he'd pressed his nose to the grindstone with such blind focus a week of PTO was waiting for him like a surprise. With a small army secured to help with the boys and seven days free, Tyler hopped on the first plane, rented a truck, and snaked through backroads and hill country while holding a Garmin GPS until at last he stood in a field.

Before him was a rugged RV. It was one of those that could have been wheeled off a Hollywood set; some movie about hillbillies or meth dealers…or a vet who'd surrounded himself by tall trees, teeming green, who'd made a clearing his home and rushed out the door to give Tyler a hug.

"You made it!"

Tyler broke free and happily gulped for air. "I have. Man, this place is something."

"It really is. Let me give you the tour." And with that, still giggling, picking right back up where they'd left off, the two walked; talking in bursts about Iraq, and Battalion, and odd jokes that occurred to them like the birds that kept flying out of the grass. Solar ovens and kettlebells were strewn about, and a bunch of logs were stacked like a pyramid near a well-used fire pit. Murray looked like a lion with his mane and shaggy hair blowing gold in the wind.

Before long a true surprise trotted out to join them. Turned out, Murray was married. She was blonde and tan as he was, in a sundress with her hair in braids. He and his wife looked like fitness models; models who skinned game and grew "magic mushrooms" and lived off his VA benefits as they potted plants and meditated out in the sun.

She said to Tyler she'd heard all about him. There was a cot in the RV with his name on it, and they were working through their wild berry larder and he would have to help them by stuffing his face. She stole him away, leaving Murray to his own desires—which Tyler half-suspected was to go run through the flowers and after climb a tree.

The inside of the RV was hilariously like the trailers of Camp Fallujah: white walls and a window unit, belting out air conditioning that Wild Man Murray apparently wasn't ready to abandon when he'd thrown away the creature comforts of civilization.

Tyler sat on an old La-Z-Boy and the two plopped down on the loveseat; separated only by a redwood coffee table that was sparkling clean. From the walls hung antlers and amateur but remarkably good oil paintings that Murray said were his wife's. They were of the various landscapes they'd seen since embarking on this adventure, he'd said, and Tyler could see now how far they'd sojourned. The usuals were there: the Grand Canyon, Niagara Falls, but he had to ask about some of the others. He was truthful when he told them his favorite was a depiction of Methuselah, explained to be the oldest tree alive.

"Oh my god," she suddenly said to Murray, "you *are not* cleaning that in here."

Murray had whipped out, seemingly from nowhere, a critter he explained he'd caught in one of his traps. It was furry and brown and dead as a doornail, and what species it was Tyler did not know or ask. He just laughed when Murray's wife excused herself from the tiny living room and took two steps away, into the kitchen, where tea was soon brewing.

The coffee table now had a rag over it and splayed out on it was Murray's catch. He held a knife. "Holistic," he said to his old team leader. "Individualistic," he cut into the carcass, slicing a line from chest to tail. "Present-minded, and out here in nature. We can't ask for more." Murray pulled a bowl out from under the loveseat while Tyler looked at the guns stacked in a corner; the ones Murray used to shoot the deer that he and his wife said they harvested year-round.

"Murr', how'd you know my address?"

Guts were being placed in the bowl. "We were on our way up to Eureka when I chucked my phone. Not long after, I realized I didn't have any of your stuff written down. I always remembered Grass's cell—all the 3s, I guess. Anyway, I called him and asked for your mailing address." Murray wiped his hands. "But he didn't know it either."

Tyler remembered then the text he'd received from Grass, asking for his address, probably on that same evening. Tyler remembered wondering at the time what on earth was going on, but such questions were forgotten in a deluge of HR meetings.

Murray laughed, "I swore Grass to secrecy. I invited him up here too, but he'd said the timing wasn't right, or something. But anyway, here *you* are." Murray was sawing the thing's neck now, seemingly with some difficulty, "The man himself."

"Wait a minute," Tyler said, "Why'd you ask for my address? Why not my phone number, or you could have maybe just emailed me."

"Yeah, but you gotta admit," the little brown head popped free, rolling onto the floor, "the snail mail was way more rustic." Murray laughed. Tyler laughed too, tempted to pull his feet up onto the recliner.

In the days that followed, they would hike the hills, rucks

on their backs nowhere as heavy as the recon days. Tyler held a rifle again and trailed behind Murray through the trees and heather very much like they were on patrol again. Under the teachings of Murray, Tyler bagged his first and only deer, afterward replicating what had been done on the coffee table, though much larger in scale and far messier. He insisted he do the cutting, and Murray showed him where to place the blade as if teaching a new teammate the ins and outs of a radio.

Murray never said why he'd invited Tyler. The strange thing was they talked so little. They spoke of small things and of the heavy things; like who had died and who had gone on to do what, but much of their time was spent in silence.

"Did you invite me here so I could see how you live now?" Tyler eventually asked. Murray rose each morning with the sun, rinsing with a bucket out by the logs. After he'd go on a run, and there were a few mornings where Tyler joined him. They swung kettlebells and so too did Murray's wife; exceptionally fit and used to the workouts that showed Tyler exactly how out of the Marine Corps he'd truly become.

"I never went to the VA for anything once I got my rating," Murray said. It was Tyler's last night. Murray's wife had made tea again, this time laced with magic mushrooms she'd crushed and ground down with a wooden pestle. "I haven't watched the news in years and hurled my last cell phone off the Golden Gate Bridge."

They hadn't drank that tea yet, and Tyler had to ask what it was like to live without a job. At the moment, the prospect of it was feeling like paradise.

"No, we work," Murray said, nodding to his better half as she handed him his cup and took a sip of her own. "She teaches biology at two different colleges—online, of course. When the semester opens back up we'll move to a place with Wi-Fi. As for me, I run a wilderness survival course out here: a sort of reclaim your manhood thing. We do it six times a year. God knows they need it. The money ain't bad, plus I like helping those types of guys."

"Ever get any vets out here? To *reclaim their manhood?*"

"Not a one," Murray said, looking Tyler in the eyes. And there Murray stated what Tyler came to believe was the real point of this trip: "I think we never lost ours."

Tyler declined the shroom tea, but he chomped down on the venison he'd earned, earned with the first shot he'd fired since having returned from Iraq.

And so the war began. And so the retaking of Fallujah began, starting where the team could hardly imagine.

"Benchmark 42!?" Murray cried.

"That's right," Grass spit. "Benchmark fuckin' 42."

All morning, Murray had been beside himself. "If the war was on the sun," he said, making despairing gestures toward the city, "this place is near the dark side of freakin' Pluto."

Murray and Grass were right, more or less, and their frustrations were felt by everyone. The dismal hill was further away from Fallujah than could be reached by the stoutest rifle.

Worse yet, the team was stuck with every clerk and field grade officer the eye could see. The hill was a light and boring brown, and on its low, barren summit sat dozens of their Humvees. All were parked and turned off. A few five-ton trucks added to the menagerie; loaded with water jugs and crates of MREs, looking like elephants amidst a herd of lesser creatures, all doomed to rot on the sand.

"I thought we were supposed to be the *mascot*," Murray rolled his eyes. "What, they pin some medals on us and then wake up today thinking we're scared?" Murray slapped the handguards of his M4. "Every second that passes that battle gets that much closer to being over."

Grass said, sounding far away, "We need to be in there, like everyone else."

"It's not fair," Jim said, "to us or to them."

Bags had tried to numb himself by watching the few comm guys erect and stake down the battalion's main antenna, but now he was squinting toward Fallujah. To the north he could make out the dim shapes of personnel carriers, a whole convoy of them, still crawling their way toward the city. He listened and thought he heard gunshots, but they were so faint he may have imagined them.

Grunts by the hundreds were infiltrating the city, and every other platoon in Battalion was steadily on their way to join them: going to Insert Alpha and Bravo and what the hell ever. Here, the team of four and the rest of their sulking platoon were apparently destined to be far away. Bags searched for Carmichael or Gunny Ulfe when he turned to see Grass approaching. The old man and Gunny were nowhere to be found; hopefully behind a five-ton, shaking the battalion commander by the shoulders, demanding no platoon of Recon Marines deserved to be security for headquarters in a moment such as this.

"Smoke?" Grass said. Bags readily accepted.

Bags had seen personnel carriers before, and he couldn't help but wonder if those tan eight-wheelers were the exact same ones he'd seen back in Lejeune.

It had been late one evening when autumn was raging and the tank trails were perfect for a run. No one was out there at that time of night, save for the deer and the lone Recon Marine who'd tightened his shoes and set out from the barracks.

Somewhere around Mile Hammock Bay it happened, the carriers and how they wheeled out of the starry blackness to pass Bags on his left-hand side. He counted four and though he couldn't see if anyone was in them, he imagined them loaded with troops, grunts most likely, on their way to some LZ to maybe set camp and train on how to keep perimeters secure.

As the carriers growled down the tank trail, sand-colored behemoths on that lighter ribbon of white, something struck Bags that he had to run faster. A bout of watching the news that evening had shown record numbers of dropouts, a wave of death in the Southeast and upstate New York. As he ran he pictured the men in the carriers as coming from those places, sidestepping deaths and dropping out, and the sad Americana he now had to escape with his very feet.

He didn't know why he sometimes thought of such things. Some back in the barracks would have called him maudlin, over intellectual, negative, if they'd known such words. All he knew was that when such things entered his mind, they did like an invading army, and they would be with him until he shook each and every last one out of his ear. This night; running was the way.

And so he ran, ran like he'd never stop. Ran until he felt he was about to burst out of his shoes, his skin, his life, the world.

At some point, the personnel carriers having long disappeared, he turned around and began making his way back. He was still fresh and his heart pounded. The air was an autumn's cool, though sweat poured off his brow.

His thoughts were digging backward too.

One of the skateboarders back in his teen years had avoided the pills and instead had found religion. He still skated, and he still cussed, just his curse words were fewer, and he started going to concerts for bands like Five Iron Frenzy. There had been kids who had especially evangelical parents back during baseball, but their talk merely mimicked those who tucked them in at night. But this kid had been different. There had come those jabs his way; that once God was found the boredom would soon follow. No more would be aggression, or free thought, or raised fists to duke it out with another of God's children. But the older skater was different. He remained one of the most brazen on the halfpipe. He baffled those who thought opening the bible meant closing the mind, for he soon questioned the cosmos, our place in it, and rose his fists more than once to the already-drug-addicted punks who called him names.

This guy had laughed about the arguments he'd got into in school. He'd said he'd been reading "apologetics" and wanted to sharpen his iron against others, and how most just called him fascist. This skater had told a story once of how a girl whom he'd broken up with had called him months later to say she was reading *Mere Christianity* on the beach. And then one day, a semester into college, he'd confided in Tyler Boggs that he'd lost his faith.

Bags ran, and as he did his thoughts remained on his old friend, who'd died of heroin. Sand and broken shell were under his shoes, and he wondered what the guy had run up against while in college; what had stripped him of his beliefs so quickly. And what, if anything, had replaced it. Images of professors came next, professing, saying in so many words that gods and faiths were all outdated, and the only faith left was to be put in articulated, rational Man.

How many of his fellow Americans had done this? Bowed to the new idol of the human will? How many had traded the idea of heaven after death for utopia on earth? And how much hopelessness in the West had derived from it?

The lights from the third deck of the barracks were close now, seen through a split in the trees. Bags ran, feeling the acid in his legs. Solo runs were the one place where his thoughts were entirely his own. There, in the night, unburdened by the duties of being a member of a team, the boy who became the man and the man who'd once been the boy were one and the same. And, knowing that in a few moments more he would be Corporal Boggs, one final thought flitted through his head and was gone.

He ran as if to fly free, and perhaps so many others sought the same thing. So many sought their liberation through the plunging sting of a needle, faceless women whose names were washed away with the sheets, or through the bottle that never gave back.

In the beginning, and perhaps in the end, everyone stood on a launch pad. And he hoped that those who crashed and burned would at least be remembered.

"We're moving toward the city," said Gunny Ulfe. A moment prior, he had stepped out of his Humvee, shutting the door, and tightened his helmet's chinstrap. Now the platoon looked at him as if stunned. Carmichael was at his side.

"Moving, like moving now, Gunny?" Bags had stuttered it more than he'd asked. They'd just spent all that previous day and a red sunrise accepting their fate. The battalion commander had been seen lounging on the hood of what some jokingly referred to as Humvee One. He'd been finishing off an MRE like a man content on a camping trip. Then he was off the hood, glued to his radio and reportedly talking to some general. The ant pile was soon stirred, and the stick of war sent Benchmark 42 into a frenzy. Now, with the ending of a single radio transmission, Gunny stood in full kit, eyes to the north.

"Now, Corporal," he said, but to the whole platoon. Bags and Jim, Murray and Grass, they felt their gear suddenly grow heavy. There were certainly dangers that came with not entering Fallujah; damages that came in the forms of boredom and shame. But shame did not rip through the flesh, nor did boredom blow out the back of one's skull.

Murray wore a smile, but it was cold and fading. No words were needed; his eyes spoke for everyone. They were going in, into the city, into "the breach" Bags thought, though he couldn't remember where that line had come from.

A further surprise came when Jim turned toward their Humvee and Gunny called him back. "We aren't taking any vehicles, Corporal James," Gunny said. They would be making their way on foot: "Dealing with enemy along the way," their platoon sergeant added, "though chances are high anyone with a stomach for fighting is already in the city."

LT came up from behind, who for days had been so mired in meetings with higher-ups that this was a minor resurrection. "Gunny," he ordered, spinning heads, "move 'em out."

And soon, all those destined to remain on Benchmark 42 watched as the platoon departed, descending onto the low ground. Bags watched Carmichael when LT took the lead, the tip of the spear, and how the old man's eye twinkled. Behind the lieutenant walked Gunny Ulfe, whose shorter, more muscular frame became a black silhouette next to their leader's as the two walked into the sun. The four teams needed no plan; they formed the trailing wings of this great V, in time fanning out so far the rear men on both sides could hardly see LT, or Gunny, or the reporter Carmichael, who walked alongside Gunny; notepad in hand.

Above them all burned that bright and unobstructed sun, though its heat was not what it had once been; when the Marines had first arrived.

More roads and berms than could be counted lay between them and their fate, their destiny, and up and over them the platoon went. LT would halt when he thought he'd spotted an IED, and so too would team leaders and members of the teams as they themselves crossed the sandy paths and hardball out on the flanks. All the while, Murray and the other radio operators kept the platoon as one mind, passing sitreps on to LT and any word from him back down to the teams themselves.

At the team level, the men talked freely, as Bags did with Jim, who was just far enough ahead so that Bags shouted into an irregular Iraqi wind.

"Freakin' sandstorm," yelled Bags.

"And just the perfect time." Jim, a stone's throw up front, now hacked and gagged. He spat out a sample of sand and dirt that had been carried by the air. "Patrol to Fallujah, and when we get there our rifles'll be filthy. Probably won't shoot…"

Jim's griping trailed off, muffled by the wind, and as it did Bags squinted and cast his eyes north. He hadn't been able to see the city, but now this sudden onset made it so that he could hardly see a football field ahead. Sandstorms came and went, and of course, one would blanket them now.

While on patrol—no—this was no patrol, this was an insert. No different than jumping out of a plane, his platoon was conducting the wartime simplicity of getting from A to B. It was safer to insert under the cover of darkness, using night-vision goggles that the enemy hopefully didn't have. It was easier to insert when sand wasn't in your eyes, when your rucks weren't laden with more water and ammunition than you'd ever carried in your life. But this was the way of it, squinting, holding your weapon with both hands and shrugging your ruck, sucking sand that came like God's own joke as you and your brothers made the long march.

Whether it was Desert Storm, the African theater with Patton, or the hallowed shores of Tripoli, sand was always there. A bland, nothing-like element of military campaigns, until, that is, it needed dug out of a fighting hole or was used to fill the green or gray bags that would soon stop enemy bullets. Then it was everywhere.

In the movies, soldiers always looked dirty. The good movies, anyhow. But for all the fake blood and fake sweat and grimy uniforms that looked about to rot off gym-toned shoulders, no actor's face ever showed what those who lived it all knew; the sheer, outright misery. Not from fear of death—actors faked that quite well. But from sand in the crotch, in every nook and cranny of a rifle just cleaned, inside boots and under armpits even though you have on long sleeves and body armor. Time's ancient grains were high on the list of environmental extremes; middle fingers stuck high in the air, in the angered faces of warriors for millennia, and counting.

Sand had a way of getting in everywhere it shouldn't. Fighting holes were the worst, but Bags supposed they could at least be thankful none of those were around. That was for Marines meant to defend someplace. Not for those who were tasked with attack. Tiny, irksome grains of desert sand got in and behind his ears, labored as if self-aware until caked in his nether regions. And Jim's worry over dirty weapons could not be so easily dismissed.

From the day they'd received their rifles back in boot camp, the mythos of Marine Corps marksmanship and the ethos of a clean weapon went hand in hand. Roads were crossed and berms were walked up and down and as the miles passed, and the sand storm raged, Bags wondered how Carmichael was holding up, laughed at how bad the rest of the platoon must have been bitching, and thought how, first stop, his M4 would have to be cleaned.

Onward went the platoon, burdened by weight and flying, howling sand. The team walked closer together now, shooting wry smiles, joking how God or Allah had seen fit to pester them but at least it wasn't Benchmark 42. Their positions switched, Bags in front, then Murray, then Grass. And as fast as it came it went: the wind, dying in a gasp that left Grass's bangs blowing, then all was still.

They continued their march.

"It's so quiet," Grass said after a while.

The fields they crossed now were powdered by a fine layer, the type of sand that was more like sugar than dirt, the stuff kicked up from miles away, out where the Euphrates touched nothing, those blank places always looking on maps and slideshows as good places to die. Bags looked at all the boot prints his men were leaving, thinking how in recon days of old they may have called them a "target indicator."

People were here.

The enemy was here, some foe of theirs would have whispered.

Out here, in these fields, that were so hauntingly quiet.

They walked like four points of a diamond: Grass up front, Jim taking up the rear, Murray on the left, and Bags on the right. Murray's handset rested clipped to his chest. Suddenly, Bags saw Murray yank it free and press it up to his ear.

"Hush," Murray then said to everyone, though no one was

talking. Then they all watched as he stopped and listened. Turned out, much had happened as the sandstorm ended, and Fallujah was not as silent as out in the fields.

Fixed-wing aircraft, dipping in low, obliterated targets. Seemingly out of nowhere, they'd appear, all on the same west-east vector, knocking entire buildings flat. There were cave-ins, and smoke and fire. These missions were few in number, likely called in by grunt commanders who'd come across homes that had been turned into fortresses. No doors would be kicked in, not there; not if fire teams were to run nose-first only into manned anti-tank guns, barrels pointed dead at them, thousand-pound weapons bolted to the floor.

Apaches conducted gun runs, flying in pairs, above the outer stretches of the city. Mujahideen fighters from Iraq and Syria and parts unknown shouldered rocket-propelled grenade launchers, shooting up at the helicopters; all of them missing, some though coming incredibly close. The Apache pilots zig-zagged, narrowly avoiding the projectiles, delivering automatic death to the enemy on the ground; maybe in windows, maybe running for their lives.

All this Bags learned from Murray, who yelled excitedly what was being said over the radio. Jim and Grass listened too, shrinking their dispersion as Murray relayed word for word the chaos that was unfolding.

There was more.

A flurry of mortar missions had just come in. Grunts were well within the city and had set up and now death was *thoon-king* out of mortar tubes, landing god knows where. Murray's excitement cooled when reports came in about men with sniper rifles, fearsome adversaries hidden in bush and window, on the roofs of houses yet to be obliterated, under cars, looking through their glass, delivering their accuracy.

"Let's keep moving," Bags said. They all looked at him and nodded. Bags took point, Jim followed, and when Murray took the rear this time nobody needed to hear his radio. He must have sensed it, for he kept his handset against his ear as they walked, but he said nothing.

An hour later they still couldn't see Fallujah. "How far south are we," they all said in their own ways. Bags consulted his AL FALLUJAH map, still out in front and shaking his head. It just didn't seem that far on paper. He stuffed the map back down his cargo pocket. To their right, they could see other platoon mates: smaller than G.I. Joes with the renewed distance now between the teams. To the left there was nothing.

"What's that?" Grass said. They all looked and saw he was pointing to something out in the field. About midway from the road they needed to cross and the berm on which they stood, there was something lying in the dirt. It was white and not terribly big, closer in size to a dug-up rock than the headstone Bags started to envision as they made their approach.

"LT's saying we're stopping in another klick," Murray announced. "Says there's some sort of wall he wants us to all meet under."

That must have meant some good cover was ahead, maybe some decent shade too. Now that the sand was done and the wind was gone, the sun was back. Not that noon against a wall would do much good, but maybe palms would be shading the area. In this part of the farmlands, they grew sporadically, but big ones were in no short supply. The team eyed the dim outline of trees up ahead, and as they did they continued toward the white thing in the dirt.

Perhaps his eyes were better than even Bags had known, or perhaps a keen intuition had served him. "Weird," he said. At the toe of his boot, there lay a skeleton.

"Where's the rest of 'em?" Jim asked, wincing a little.

"Murray said, "Here…and *there*," using the toe of his own boot to unearth more bones.

They stared down at the femurs, a pelvis, the ribcage with sun-bleached cloth still clinging to it. And they stared at a white shiny skull; what Grass had seen from the berm.

"I can't tell if it's man or woman," Jim said.

Bags bent down. "None of us can, Jim." Bags examined the cloth. It was of that kind so popular out there, the type of gray that could be a man's shirt or once a woman's dress, or had once been jet black until time under the sun had made it lighten and wither. One thing was for sure, it had been picked clean. Word was there were jackals out here. Rats had been seen in a house or two, and every battlefield on earth held its flies. All carrion, whomever they'd been, were gone now; leaving only a skeleton that Bags couldn't identify as Iraqi or one of the few American service members who were currently missing.

It was a strange thing to have recently killed men yet be so transfixed by death. Or maybe it wasn't. Bags asked Murray to report their find to Gunny and LT, and after this he said no more. He kept his mouth shut, knowing no one in the team, not even dear Jim, would understand. A sappy poet, maybe so, but he couldn't shake the thought of death. Weeds grew near the bones and he imagined a sickly process of decay, rot: the final destination.

"Yo, you hear what I said?"

Bags looked up to see Murray staring at him. "Yes…"

Murray smirked, "Gunny said leave it. If it's American, well—"

Bags stood. "If it's American?"

"If he was an American," Murray said, "he has far less to worry about now than *we* do. Gunny said get the coordinates and LT will call it in."

Bags pulled out his Garmin, recording where they stood. He tossed the GPS to Murray and Murray read off the coordinates into the radio. As he did, Bags turned to Jim.

"Whoever they were," he said, soberly, "all their life, just to end up bones in a field."

"I wouldn't look at it that way," Jim said. "Not if you can help it."

Another hour passed and they were sitting along the south side of LT's wall. It was made of cinder block and unpainted and tall as a man. They'd been there for some minutes, half the platoon was cleaning the sand from their weapons as the other half stood watch. There were trees overhead, but not the stout palms Bags had hoped for. Above them stretched branches out of a bad fairy tale, leafless twigs from bent trunks reaching out like fingers. The trunks themselves, close enough to the wall, provided a spit of shade the Marines gathered under.

"I've seen hotter days," said Grass, adjusting under a shadow. "But mama didn't raise a fool." He passed a cleaning rag to Bags.

"Yeah," said Bags. "Probably the last bit of shade we'll get until we're inside."

Murray laughed. "Yeah, and you can imagine once in the

city we won't be doing much sitting."

Everyone in the team had looked for Carmichael. When they'd spotted him he'd been against the wall, hidden by LT and Gunny. The old man eventually broke away from the leaders and made his way about the teams. Bags watched as he weaved within the platoon, smiling to those on the step of war, offering kind words. The last team he came to was theirs.

"I see none of you were blown away by the sand," he said, standing over the team as they finished.

"Nope," Grass said, "now we get to get blown away by something else." Some laughed. Others didn't.

Carmichael frowned. "If anyone has a chance of surviving, surely it's you."

"Yeah, Grass," Jim said. "Can we keep the doomsday talk down? I'm scared enough as is."

"Scared?" Grass said.

"And better is he for admitting it," Carmichael looked at Grass, at them all.

They all knew Grass was scared, too. They all were. As they were excited, excited by knowing they were soon to go beyond the threshold, into the unknown. They were ready, and they weren't. They imagined everyone dying but them— the thought of their own simply something their minds couldn't bend around. It was an ancient reaction perhaps, felt by all men who held their breath before taking that great plunge.

An explosion then rang through everyone's ears. It had come over the wall but its origin had been far away. The dull roar was soon explained by Gunny as friendly artillery rounds, devastating some target.

Carmichael walked toward the wall now. Gunny had one

hand on its cinder block, standing on his toes. The team was on their feet, M4s reassembled and clean enough, and they joined Gunny and Carmichael and peaked over. Veiled by smoke and remnants of the storm still blowing brown in the breeze, they saw in the distance the roofs of Fallujah.

"Okay," Gunny said, one ear to his handset. "Our platoon is now being told to go ahead and push to the city, seven blocks in once we insert."

"Insert Bravo?" Bags asked, knowing the answer. The wall they stood behind stretched to their left and right, but shorter to their left. The platoon was now completely on its feet, and they began a single-file march; going around the left side.

LT was soon out in front, talking with Carmichael and pointing to the north. Gunny Ulfe, who was walking next to Bags and still listening to his radio, lowered his handset and said, "Go ahead and take point, Bags. Karl was insisting he be up there with you. We stop when we get to the Row of Four."

There were no more questions. Every man in the platoon, from Bags to Jim to the comm guy to Hendershot, knew theirs was to march north and climb to the tops of four buildings to support grunts for as long as the shit show lasted and hopefully not die.

No one knew what that wall and its many cinder blocks had been built for. There was no aqueduct. It didn't enshrine the oasis of a thriving green field. It didn't seem to serve as much of anything other than a convenient obstacle along the way. But, to a man, once northward that wall, the platoon felt the whole country change.

Facing them, the smallest farmhouse stood. No need for radios. This they'd practiced so many times they could do it deafened and blindfolded. As Bags and his team were making their way forward, LT motioned for one team to plant itself out front and for everyone else to continue along the house's right side. Everyone except for the team charged with clearing it.

And the change was soon felt.

Though Bags and his men were now the foremost team, they were not who infiltrated, nor were they the guys steadying themselves to provide a base of fire in case enemy shooters were within. Bags and his team skirted around the little house, and as they did he listened to his radio. Not a soul was left in the place, it was soon reported, and now other threats came upon their path; cars, trucks, new little houses; all abandoned. One truck had its keys still dangling in its ignition. Another had both of its doors open, as if ghosts had flown from its passenger and driver's seats. Onward they marched; toward new threats, new abandoned houses, and no Iraqis were seen here, not even a lone on-looker braving a peek through a window.

Bags couldn't help but think of a paper he'd written back in high school about the Sahara. How on its north and southern edges life could live, but its middle-most section was almost entirely barren. Here something similar passed underneath his boots. They'd left the places where people dwelled, and to people they were returning, but now they traversed this nether realm. It was as if a great hand had reached down and squeezed them right out of existence, leaving only a farmland full of whispers.

"Duck and cover!" someone yelled.

The platoon was stretched out in a long file. Those up front with Bags turned, and in a brief flash stared quizzically The cry had come from their rear. Carmichael turned too, and as he did they all watched Gunny and Hendershot and a few others run and dive in a ditch.

A fountain of dirt erupted, right where Bags and his team had walked a minute before. Right before this newest threat had impacted, a searing falling sound had torn through the air. Then there was the explosion and the dirt and smoke, followed by a concussion Bags felt in his lungs as he gripped tighter his rifle and swung to see LT screaming in his radio.

It was a bad fire mission, shot from a howitzer back in Camp Fallujah. Gunny popped out of the ditch, joining the lieutenant on a different radio frequency.

Bags had first thought, as did every man in the platoon, that the enemy had fired a mammoth round. It was not easy to hear everything LT and Gunny were now saying. They were on opposing ends of the platoon's sprawled-out patrol, but both were chewing the ass of some fire direction officer. The shell had torn out a chunk of earth and its smoke was still smoldering and it had simply been an errant round; one the fire direction officer was busily apologizing over.

Bags chuckled as the patrol began dusting itself off. Bags

knew that FDO would hang up and storm over to chew the asses of the entire gun line. Shit rolled downhill, and even in times of war, the human ego would demand its seat at the table. The patrol resumed, a little more cautiously now, Bags's team out front, with a little more ear to the wind.

Before long, after traversing more brown and green and dirt and grass, another small house stood between them and Fallujah.

"Bags," LT said over the radio, "You're up."

Jim and Grass were already moving, stacking alongside the wall by the front door. Soon the stack was Grass, Jim, Murray, then Bags—who then squeezed Murray's shoulder; initiating a chain until Jim's hand squeezed Grass, and Grass was through the door.

They flowed in, like armored water, stopping only once in their appointed points of domination; this corner of the living room—which was barren—and that corner, and the next corner, until all was secure.

The house was a simple square. In the living room, they saw open doorways to what were probably bedrooms to the left and right. Murray and Grass went through one, Jim and Bags went through another. Soon both teams were yelling "Clear!" and, after, converging again in the living room.

"Looks to be a kitchen back here," Jim now said. He stood at the deepest corner, peering around the last doorless entrance, one that led to the back of the house. Bags made his way over to Jim, and as he did, a sound came from beyond where Jim was looking. It was perhaps a pan that fell, hitting the floor with a metallic smack and rattle, but it was enough to make everyone's rifle go up. Someone was in here.

"Jim," Bags said, "what do you see?"

"Nothin'," said Jim, rifle up. "I can't see far around." This was the case in many Iraqi houses. The walls without doors just sort of ended, leaving a warfighter with a limited view of what waited on the other side.

Murray and Grass had moved to Bags' side. Bags was behind Jim, and he gave Jim the squeeze.

All four Marines went into the kitchen, a breach of procedure, but none were going to miss out. A cat stared at the four then darted behind a cupboard, knocking over another pan for its troubles.

"All clear," Bags said into his radio. He spun to see a stairway. *Well*, he thought, *maybe not*. He pointed and they moved, single-filing it up the short spiral staircase until they saw the blue sky above.

As they made their way up onto the roof, it dawned on Bags that this would *not* be the only stairs they would be climbing. He imagined the ones in the Row of Four, but being littered with bodies, covered in the warm slip of blood. As they stood on the roof and waved to Gunny, Bags looked out at the platoon and wondered who among them would not be with them much longer.

"Check this out, fearless leader," Murray said from behind. "What a war we're in. We're screwed, I'm afraid. Arty can't shoot and PSYOPS drops an entire pallet on a single roof." Murray stood grinning, pointing to what Bags, as he turned, realized he'd been stepping on. They were all over the place.

Some lay trampled by their boots. Some flapped in the wind. Some still were amassed in the bundle that had been dropped by a fixed wing and had failed to disperse like rain.

Having not come apart, hundreds if not thousands of leaflets were before them. The rest of the platoon looked up from the ground, one team still in their base-of-fire position while the rest strolled past. Some waved oafishly but most, to include Gunny and Carmichael, stopped to see why the four on the roof were still standing about.

Bags bent down and picked up a leaflet.

"Looks like running away can be a good time," Jim said from over his shoulder.

Bags shook his head. "How we can Disney-up a warzone is beyond me."

"Oh, you know," said Jim, "gotta win those hearts and minds, sir."

Murray and Grass began tromping back down the stairs. Jim stood with Bags for a moment then he followed them. On the well-meaning leaflets were cartoons of Iraqis, all of them, man-woman-child, all smiling, all running out of Fallujah; the city bulking black against an aquamarine sky. Their smiles were so large.

Soon, the platoon approached something like a parking lot. Houses enclosed this dirt square, and all about it were empty trucks. Not a windshield there was spared the bite of a bullet. Every window, spidered or shattered, was shot to pieces.

"Target practice?" said Jim.

Carmichael scratched his chin. "This one's tires are flat. That one's door is riddled like cheese. This was someone making sure others couldn't leave."

"Didn't seem to work," Bags remarked.

"Yeah," Jim fingered a bullet hole. "Looks like everyone up an' left anyway."

Right then a rifle fired. Though it was far to the north, some of the Marines reflexively sought cover. Among them was Bags, who took a knee near the rear of a truck and was eye-level with its license plate. Whoever had shot that rifle either had killed their target or had died. Perhaps they ran out of ammo, for the shooting had stopped.

It was a strange thing: little bits of clutter overseas had a way of carrying one away. A Coke can crushed into a certain shape, the way a man may open a particular pack of cigarettes, a license plate: all bringing one back to a different time.

Recon Marines certainly went to jump school. Running out of a plane to fall to the earth was a tradition as much as it was a method of insert, and a few lucky men even got to go to military free fall. FF meant much higher altitudes and that you had to pull your own cord. It was more *elite*, as the custom went, and no one in Bags's team had been able to go.

So they went themselves; the civilian route; stuffing into a single vehicle to attend weekend classes and soon his whole team was certified. Bags on his high knee was thinking of that time they did a series of jumps over the course of a single weekend. There was the low and steady hum of the plane. That violent roar that meets a skydiver upon their leap. Another rattle of rifle fire from that dreaded city and Bags thought of falling so fast and so low that he hadn't pulled that damn cord until he could see the license plate of his own parked car. Anything, rather than walk headfirst into where they were now going.

The platoon was on the move. LT fell back to give priority to his radio. Higher was demanding to know it all; the sights, the smells, the sounds observed on their approach to the city, all of which the battalion commander would relay to generals poised around a mapped-out table. Gunny took point, and point he stayed. Bags and his team were soon behind him, Carmichael mixed in between Jim and Murray. No one talked now. The shot-up parking lot was behind them all, and they all traversed an open field; the very last of the farmlands before the edge of the city that was coming into view. A moat of farmhouses waited for them on the far side.

Bags knew Gunny had heard him when he turned to his team and said, "These houses look like a perfect place for snipers." Grass stuck out his chin, slowing his step. Jim and Murray and even Carmichael seemed to show fear, though none spoke or lessened their stride.

But soon they were at the very last of the houses, marching through someone's side yard. The terrain was channeling them ever close to Insert Bravo. *"Bravo is straight hardball; opening up between two,"* Bags saw the tall twin roofs, a distance not so far now. He squinted and he saw the black that would be their path; a darkened slice in all that brown and gray. Their radios were silent now. They walked until the houses were at their backs, though menace still lay in every window. When Bags would turn, and he did more than once, shapes seemed to move behind those windows, just beyond the reach of fact or fantasy. Gunny had said there had been too many houses to clear, so they hadn't. If snipers lay in wait, for war's own mystery they had let the Americans pass.

Gunfire was heard, much louder now. The platoon's rifles were cold, but someone, somewhere, out to the north, was answering an AK-47 that fired, stopped, then fired again. There were exchanges of a similar kind going off all over the city, brutal one-on-ones often met with an overwhelming crack of M4s, or the morbid cacophony of AKs that won back some blood-drenched room.

That wall, now a world away behind them, had been a portal. And these houses with their ghosts in the windows, they too had been a barrier the platoon had breached. Now, the sounds of battle were near. The *ratta-tat-tats* were sometimes drowned by brief *booms*; explosions that Bags could feel run up his legs and die at his waist.

Gunny Ulfe began to run. The platoon began to run, unsure whether Gunny had been shot at or saw some target and needed cover. But they followed, thundering over a brief gap of earth until crowded against the southern wall of a tall building.

"Bravo," Jim said, panting.

"There," Bags could hardly believe his eyes. "Gunny, there's gotta be a better route."

There were two buildings before them, standing like pillars before a grand entrance. These two buildings provided enough cover for Bags to do as Carmichael and Hendershot and others did: hide. Bags peeked around a corner. All along Insert Bravo, cars had been parked on both sides. Not only that, their enemy had stacked every bit of rubbish on these cars; from trash to cinder blocks both old and new. The once-street was now an alley, a claustrophobic turkey shoot of an alley...onto which Gunny stepped toward.

"This is the only way," he said, looking back, "at least for us." Gunny then turned and fixed his eyes forward and then his foremost boot touched the black road. Bags's team was right behind him, and an explosion sent them flying.

There was an old photo Bags couldn't forget if he tried. It was of his uncle, taken by someone behind him as his uncle was stepping onto the gangplank of a swift boat. The boat is silver and the dark water it floats in is calm, eerily so. One can't see Bags's uncle's face but there is his uniform; sleeves rolled up, veins spidering down his forearms. There's a messy crop of brown hair and shiny black boots. One boot is on the wooden plank and the other still on the soil of Vietnam.

Like Bags's father, Bags's uncle had served. He'd enlisted in the Navy and ran swift boats up and down the Mekong Delta. If the citations were true, he was always on time, never missed a pickup, or shied away from danger.

Unlike his older brother, and probably a lot more like Carmichael, he saw action. As one story went, an ambush cost them three men in as many seconds and the machine gun on the bow got hit with a Russian round that sent ammo flying. Another made the portside look like "Cheese from a Tom and Jerry cartoon", though the sailors and their armed cargo decimated the riverbank so that only blood and vegetation remained.

His uncle had survived Nam, and he got out and took employment with a business that went under. His uncle said he missed the war and reenlisted days before a drunk driver slammed his spine into the driver's side of a parked car. He ended up just another long-haired vet in a wheelchair, spitting at those who mistook his misfortune for wartime deeds. He crawled for a while crippled through the furnace of America, making headlines after being arrested in a bar fight and having to be wheeled into a cornpone county jail. He was offered rehab. A nadir involving money and a fight with Bags's grandparents eventually flopped him on the doorsteps of the VA. He learned to walk again, but the pain pills became heroin. There lingered a family myth: a tale of a sad man wobbling out in the rain, screaming he'd simply learn to fly again with a syringe still stuck in his arm. Years later he would beat the needle, too, but he smoked until the day he got the diagnosis, and puffed his Pall Malls when his hair was gone.

"Grass…." The name came from the end of a long, ringing tunnel. "Grass…." Murray was bent over, rifle dangling. Murray was standing over someone—Grass—who was sitting on the road with his back against a car. He shook him, yelling if it weren't for his voice sounding so far away. "Grass!"

"Jesus!" Bags suddenly cried, his hearing coming back to him. "You guys okay?"

Jim was on a knee, busily wrapping his own hand. It was bleeding and as Jim wrapped red soaked through the bandage. Jim said, "I will be."

Bags realized he was on his ass. His legs were spread out in front of him like a *V*. He spit out sand and dust and smelled now the acrid black powder that had—

"What happened?" he said, patting himself down, checking to see if he too was bleeding. As he wobbled to his feet, Gunny hoisted him up by his collar.

"IED," Gunny growled, scanning the windows. "Someone's watching. Remote detonated."

Grass was now upright too, staring at the gaping pocket in the car that had hidden the bomb. A quarter panel had been packed with some sort of explosive; some sort of dirty bomb.

When it had gone off, the panel flowered outward; leaving only a blackened empty hole. Bags had been rocked but no flying metal had pierced him. He found that he was cussing and over his irritation he heard Gunny on the radio tell LT that Jim had taken a piece of shrapnel but was no worse for wear.

Now the rest of the platoon was flowing into Insert Bravo. Bags's team, Carmichael, Gunny—they hadn't gotten far. Now, all eyes stalked, burrowing into every window and parked car and shadow on the face of the world. Nothing stirred.

Down the hardball, Bags could see there lay a body. Two bodies. Three. All Iraqi: killed by gunfire.

LT was being swarmed so fully by demands on the radio that he stayed in the rear. He was the liaison and conduit for men who became senators and first oversaw the dropping of thousand-pound bombs. Gunny Ulfe was the man who'd seen war up close, and up close it was again. And there they stood, on the black pavement, Bags and his team and Gunny Ulfe and Carmichael without a weapon. Gunny told everyone to shake it off. He made his way past where the IED had gone off and soon took a knee behind the back tire of a truck. He checked his gear.

Carmichael and Bags's team took refuge behind a tall heap of their own and Grass lit a smoke.

"If I die," Grass exhaled, "please God make it be from cancer."

"If you bite it," said Murray, "I'll lie about your bravery. Get you another medal for Mom."

Carmichael laughed.

It was Jim's turn. "Heck," he said, "if one of you dies it'll mean the other's gone, too. You're attached at the hip."

"Which means a lot to carry!" said Grass.

"Yeah, you got that much ass in you?" Murray took the cigarette and gave it a puff.

"Hey," Grass said, as if suddenly having remembered, "we never wrote each other in our SGLIs."

Servicemembers' Group Life Insurance was a quarter of a million bucks. If one was killed overseas it all went to the wife, or if unmarried usually someone's grieving mother; one who put ornate flowers on the tomb.

"A bit too late now," said Jim, taking the cigarette with his unbloodied hand and putting it to his lips. "Well," he coughed, "if I die you two morons can have my...," a smile streaked across his round face, "the extra canteen cup they gave me at CIF. Screw you."

"That's all we're worth?" Murray said.

Carmichael's eyes bounced from one team member to the next. "You men ready?"

"Not just yet, old man." Grass now crossed his arms. "Well, Jim, if I go you can have those shorts I forgot to wash and are still stuffed somewhere in a sea bag in Lejeune. Real ripe for you."

Murray pointed his rifle toward the sky. "Well," he said, "if I must depart this wonderful world, you all may each have a porno of mine of your choosing. Naughty things, they are. Don't wish for Mom to be mailed my stash."

Jim shook his head, and as he did he handed what was left of the team's ceremonial cigarette to their team leader. "What do you wish for, Bags?"

Bags took it. Its white was almost gone; burned close to the dark yellow of the filter. Its cherry burned bright, red as the blood that had flowed from Jim's hand, and there was a drag still to be had. He let it fall. He looked up, straight at his team. He stared at the street that lay ahead, stretching like a long black ribbon. The team, they all felt the coldness of his gaze and they became cold in turn. It was time. "What I wish for?" he spoke. "That shot-up motorcycle we all fought behind. I wish for another one of those. We're going to need it, I'm afraid."

Carmichael put out the cigarette with the toe of his boot. With a hand plopped on Bags's shoulder, he said, "If *I* buy the ranch on this one, you can have my Harley."

Grass laughed. Murray and Jim laughed. Bags laughed too. Bags said, "Let's get up there with Gunny." Shouldering his M4, he led the way.

Gripping bank statements and a police report, Tyler's dad led the way into the courthouse where a restraining order was written. Money, yes, money, or lack thereof, was the evil that bore into the fissures of the Boggs family. It shimmied in and widened, cracking then exploding a once-solid rock.

Tyler's uncle had left a trail of fire, and it burned white hot when Tyler's grandparents pleaded their disabled son should be viewed not with outrage but with pity...even after breaking into the family home and stealing heirlooms and later pawning them. Tyler's dad felt *he* was being made into the bad guy—the one hard screw in the joint who viewed antebellum silver being sold for heroin not as cries for help but low-down dirty bullshit that cost the family more than money. The five hundred bucks he'd leant he knew he'd never see again either, he told his son, and that would be fine, if his growing monster of a brother would just disappear.

In some sense, Tyler Boggs enlisted in the Marine Corps to

find family. A real family. One that functioned and fought for its own. There were times while in boot camp, right before falling asleep, where he'd take inventory. No counting sheep. He would ball his fists under his green sheet then stick out an index finger: one, the most bitter fight he'd seen his parents have. The middle finger: two, the horrid fate of his sister. Ring finger next; three, some dreary memory after another. He could fill and refill that hand several times over, drifting off, while other recruits yelled drill commands in their sleep, to images of his corpse-like uncle; being told by his red-faced father to hurry up and die.

Though his uncle would recover, the junkie days tore the brothers' relationship to shreds. Loans never repaid. Outright stealing. Tyler's dad had said there comes a time when one must learn to let go of even family, and for years they did just that. Then pancreatic cancer put Tyler and his dad inside a pickup truck, then four hundred miles from home, then into a backyard with a wooden fence to make amends and to say goodbye.

Tyler's uncle had made a bonfire and the two men drank and talked, mostly about the past until one of them brought up a Western they'd watched when they were children. It was a show they'd taken in religiously, something Tyler had never known, and in the place of "Sorry" and "I love you" and "It's okay" were debates over the name of the hero's first horse. And Tyler was given a can full of beer when their lawn chairs were kicked over and the men danced around the bonfire like Wild Indians. They hooted and howled, stomping down blades of grass until Tyler jumped up and uncontrollably cried. He danced with them, and after their dancing they all fell asleep under the stars, the moon gleaming off his uncle's head.

When it was Tyler's turn to don the uniform, he did so without telling a soul until the contract was signed and he could proudly march into two different living rooms to deliver the news. This resulted in an odd party, one put on by his parents where everyone gathered once more, and once again his father was drunk.

The Delayed Entry Program had Tyler set to ship out in four months. He'd just graduated from high school and in the fledgling days of summer none of his few friends had run off yet to college. Thus, many people showed up to the backyard gathering held at his mother's. Friends were few but acquaintances many, and faces he hadn't expected to see all warmly congratulated him on his brave step toward his journey. Tiki torches were lit and his dad, though inept at all things, insisted manning the playlist, kicking off irksome but heartfelt patriotic hymns. A few mortars and it would have been the Fourth of July; beer cans opening, burgers and hotdogs sizzling on the grill. Even his sister was there, though her stay was short, her company shady, and her hug had been limp and cold. But that was life, Tyler had thought, the crazed menagerie of ups and downs, hilarious predictions and outright surprises. His father came barreling out of a corner.

It was right as his sister was leaving, Tyler recalled. The guy who'd come to "see her" had to have been twice her age; with that hard-boiled look of one who'd seen the inside of a cage. Probably her dealer, her father would later stick to, there on a barter system of blowjobs, and that night her father's battle cry held such accusations.

And it wasn't accusations alone that turned the backyard into chaos. Tyler's dad shouldered through the crowd, slurring his words and pointing his finger. It was as if he'd come out of nowhere, emerged from the azaleas or from someplace deep in his own mind where he was still unable to admit it was *he* who'd twisted his daughter's life. Reeking of booze, he dove at the man, but he tackled only the side of the house. Tyler's sister shrieked and someone said they were calling the cops.

The man and his sister were gone like smoke, leaving only Tyler and Tyler's dad (with a bleeding head) and a yard full of nervous laughter. Undeterred, yet now adjusted to be the life of the party, his dad wobbled to his feet and cried for another beer. His high spirits were met with a few people saying that they needed to go, wishing Tyler all the best as they sidled toward the gate.

It was when Tyler tried to usher his dad inside that his dad took a swing. His dad insisted that he was embarrassing him, and "What, you think you are some big man now?" For just a moment, Tyler saw his father with pure pity, a wretched clown of a creature, one who'd drank himself stupid and was perfecting his disaster. Then Tyler saw red.

His dad reared back for another, but before he could swing Tyler was on him. And *this* tackle was well-aimed. He drove his dad to the grass, climbing on top and delivering punches into the stupid drunk's forehead and mouth. Tyler's mother screamed. People fled. Hotdogs cooked themselves black until Tyler got off. Tyler's lip was bloody. Tyler's dad looked far worse.

The next day, his dad, unable to look him in the eye, told Tyler he was swearing off the booze.

And he did.

As Tyler prepped for boot camp, his dad blinked with eyes anew at a world without the bottle. Tyler had thrown out old clothes as his father emptied the liquor cabinet. When Tyler went on late-night runs, a few times his father would insist he go alongside him on a ten-speed he'd pulled from storage. Though Tyler first said no, the sad plea in the man's eyes overpowered Tyler's disgust and his rage, and the two quietly sweat together.

There were many similar changes; Budweiser was swapped out for O'Douls. It touched Tyler deeply, to see his dad confess in his own way by going fishing with non-alcoholic beer. They talked more in that summer than they had since Tyler was a boy, back in the little league days. Their reconnection resulted in his dad stopping by he and his mother's more often. And one night he rolled up on the most drastic change of all; a crappy old motorcycle.

Before flying off to meet the Marine Corps, Tyler improved the amount of push-ups and pull-ups he could do. As he did, his dad worked on watching out for drunk drivers, and leaning into the S curves near where his kids had gone to middle school.

Come the day, his father insisted Tyler sit on the back and that he'd take him to the airport. All Tyler had on him was his backpack, clothing that would be sealed away, and his windblown hair; hours away from falling onto a boot camp barber's floor. The day burned and there was a plane and later a drill instructor. They hit every red light, lurching past churches, the law offices of divorce lawyers, the fast food chains until they hit a straightaway and Dad let it rip. That bike would get sold.

O'Douls slipped to Budweiser for one night then metastasized to Budweiser forever again. But before his father lost his battle, there was their ride.

And something happens at high speeds.

Around 80 miles an hour even a summer's wind blows cold, engines growl with the lust of an animal that carries your very life on its back, all else becomes as statues and you are no longer riding, you are flying. Wings are with you. Empty churches, offices, a crowded Mickey D's—just clutter toppling in the wake of your flight. That day they rode together, Tyler's father clutching the handlebars and Tyler clutching his waist. All their problems, all their differences, for that brief moment were all gone. Maybe Tyler's dad was holding on for as long as he could, riding faster and longer with each passing night as he felt his enemy grow. Maybe he knew a great fight was before him the moment his son left. And maybe that was the lesson for Tyler, to understand there is a war for each to fight. An enemy who wants us dead. A battle before us we may or may not win. And, in the end, we all have to face it.

Bags was over Gunny Ulfe's shoulder, and he looked out as far as he could. He looked down the now-tight alley of Insert Bravo. There were all the cars, packed on the left and right of the road with their noses or ass ends inches from the walls. Still smelling like something burned, close to them was the vehicle with the blown-out quarter panel, the one that had exploded and had bloodied Jim's hand. Up close, it had a tuna can look; that serrated, shark tooth edging more like a cartoon than a grim appendage of war. Farther down, there was all that trash, scraped and heaped by a desperate enemy. What other horrors lay in wait under burlap sacks and empty water bottles the Marines would soon know. Bags eyed once more the little black windows that loomed over where they now stood. No faces. No phones.

Gunny was on his feet, and slipping around their cover Bags and he were on the move. The plan was simple. One advantage the enemy had given them was that while the vehicles choked the road into a deadly funnel, they also provided un-expected protection. If not laced with IEDs of their own, one vehicle after the next would be how the platoon would bound. How they'd push in deeper, one backed-in truck at a time. And they did just that; Gunny taking the left of the road and Bags taking the right; Gunny moving first with half the platoon flowing in behind him in a file; Bags moving second with the other half trailing his lead while Gunny and his guys provided their cover.

Once inside the city, they stood at the foot of the three dead. The Iraqis must have had certainly met with a fire team of grunts. One Iraqi still clutched an AK, the other an RPG. The third, smaller than the other two, must have been something like an A-gunner. He lay, stomach to the sky, arched over a backpack full of rockets with his mouth open; his final moments looking to have ended in great agony.

"They should have collected these weapons," Gunny said, *they* meaning the grunts, and though he'd spoken to himself Bags heard him.

"Maybe they had other targets to worry about?" Bags called over. Gunny Ulfe nodded and got on the radio. Someone toward the rear could collect them and blow them with a pinch of C4. Bags understood the logic: destroy any weapon that the enemy could pick back up and point their way. LT's voice came over the radio, though this time Bags didn't hear what was said.

All about them, above the hoods of the cars and trucks along their path stood frowning two-story buildings. Sand-swept brown or gray as a tomb, the dreariness of the city was interrupted by brief riots of color—a red Coca Cola sign, blue tarps—some of them not shot up and others untethered, ready to flap if there'd been a wind. And brief moments of green—what Bags now strained his eyes to see; rugged, renegade plants, hedges now neglected, a lone and ill-watered tree, some gardener's project still deepening its roots while its planter lay somewhere dead.

"I've never seen a dead person before." Jim said at Bags's side. "Well, one that we didn't...you know."

"Me either," Bags said, turning away from the three dead Iraqi's and their decimated faces, thinking as he did that if he or Jim were shot in their face that somehow they wouldn't look as bad. It was a strange thing, seeing the brains and bits of bone housed behind another's eyes. All that struggle, all that beauty and wonder and regret and contemplation, seen from a place that a few bullets could open up and mutilate. *Life*, Bags laughed to himself wryly; *just a ghost, a fog that danced on all that pink and red and bone-white mess.* And it was time to move.

Soon they passed a gas station. Before they did, each and every member of the platoon snuck around one of two pumps, cringing that an especially nasty IED was about to go off and send the whole place up in flames.

"Say," said Jim, a little farther back now, "shouldn't we be gettin' closer to that Row?"

Bags had been looking directly ahead, thinking the same thing. A large building bulked gray and ruined before them. All around were the sounds of guns. The air smelled like things burning, mixed with the sand and grit odor Bags had gotten so used to but now seemed to take in as if he'd just stepped off the plane. As the staggered column patrolled northward on Insert Bravo, it was as if skirmishes were going on all about them—just out of reach, hiding behind smoldering houses and the big building they approached.

Their route put them on the right side of this building, and as Gunny and Bags skirted past its empty windows Gunny suddenly signaled for a halt. With his arm raised, hand made into a fist, Bags and the entire platoon went on a knee.

Gunny Ulfe was to Bags's left and a bit ahead, and he went onto his belly. This sent a ripple through the platoon; starting with Bags and Jim and the Marine behind Gunny. The men behind Bags must've seen how he responded, for he heard them getting low onto the pavement. Bags was on his belly, swinging his head from left to right, gun forward as he kept putting his eye back on Gunny, wondering.

But Bags didn't have to wonder for long. Their platoon sergeant had located a trip wire, and once Bags saw it he saw the entire makeup of the trap. A copper wire ran from a nail in the wall, tight and over the sidewalk that Gunny lay on, ending somewhere in the wheel well of a parked car. The wire was as long as the sidewalk was wide, maybe five feet, and all Bags could think of was Gunny skirting around the damn car and leaving the dreaded thing be.

But Gunny had already reached for his Gerber. Bags watched, remembering also that it was his duty to pull security. And though he tried he kept coming back to Gunny, watching as Gunny made ready the little wire cutters. He slithered closer.

Bags cringed as Gunny reached for the wire, breathing a sigh when he saw how the wire went limp. It lay on the concrete, cut in two, and as Gunny rose everyone followed. He radioed to LT and they were again moving.

After a time, Bags looked back and saw that Gunny's side was indeed avoiding the space between the wall and the car. One Marine spit in that direction. Another gave it the bird. Gunny and Bags put the dead trap further to their rear.

What had been weapons firing was now weapons firing amidst glass that was shattering out onto empty streets. A door slammed way too close. There were distant cries of men—not all of them in English. Insert Bravo was leading them now toward something like a town square, and among its rubble and shell casings dead dogs lay about; one with its head half-shot off. What was left snarled up in a permanent sneer.

What is up with these guns?! Bags thought. Every skirmish in Fallujah had just ended, as if called off by some maestro tired of the noise. Now the platoon walked in silence, a dead quiet save for the jingle of gear and the stepping of their boots. Maybe the skirmishes weren't so individual after all. Perhaps some leader such as Gunny was on the horn and marshaling his grunts with an iron fist. Or maybe the Muj had just all surrendered in mass, coming out arms-up to the grunts. Or maybe the grunts had all just died.

In this silence, Bags craned his neck to look at Murray, Grass, and Jim. Like the Marines farther behind them, they weren't looking at Bags at all, but up at rooftops and over into choked alleyways until they met his eyes. They all seem to nod, in unison as if rehearsed outside the shoot houses of Camp Lejeune. He was thinking of his uncle's black-and-white photo, and he knew each man in his team had a photograph of their own.

Murray's father: standing on a dune during the build-up for Desert Storm. Grass's dad had been in Nam. Grass had spoken of a war correspondent who'd captured the moment his dad went squirming into a tunnel. Jim's grandfather was killed in Korea, and he carried with him a photo of that Arlington grave.

As the platoon pushed deeper, walking quietly and steady, Bags wondered if his guys were thinking of the men in those photos: what he and his team may say to them.

"Dad, my war is deadlier than yours?"

"You crawled through tunnels and now we walk through streets?"

"I may fly to you by lunchtime."

As if prompted by Bags's thought, Jim pulled out his dog tags. Out from behind his flak jacket, and the armor plate within, his sweat-stained desert blouse and his olive-drab undershirt, the dog tags had rested. There was a cross on the necklace, too; small and silver and gleaming in the sun. Jim kissed it then stuffed it back behind his gear. Then he said, "That's the Row, isn't it?" There they were. Up ahead, over and above the squat skyline, there they loomed. Bags and Jim saw just the tops of them, four flat roofs not far away now. The Row of Four.

"It is, Jim," Bags said, now facing ahead and eyeing Gunny. What lay before them was something out of a machine gunner's dream—an enemy machine gunner's. There was the Row of Four all right, just as had been reported, four strong buildings all bunched together. The pavement the Marines were on ended at their porticos, but before a Marine could get to them a veritable tunnel awaited. *Not just a machine gunner's dream*, Bags thought, feeling his heart go to his throat, *a sniper's too.*

In another hundred feet or so, the defiled town square would end and so would begin a ghastly stretch. Their route widened some here, though their plight was no less perilous. On both sides of the road, there were no longer cars and trucks, but walls with black windows. These buildings that sealed their approach were not as high as the Row, but they were just tall enough to make the whole thing look more like a canyon than a road. The walls, cliffs, the black pavement: it was a deathly river, and it flowed north.

If the platoon were to march down Insert Bravo, they would be fish in a barrel. If every man in the platoon picked two windows and eyed them with the utmost lethality, even if Carmichael's battlefield wisdom took care of another five or six, there would still be windows unwatched. Unguarded. Unable to see immediately if a barrel poked out. And then there were the roofs; perfect places for hell to come raining down as they scrambled for what little cover could be seen.

"We aren't actually going in there, are we?" said Jim.

Bags watched Gunny. He was on the radio, and from what whispers Bags could pick up he was talking to LT and repeating in his own manner Jim's nervous question.

"I don't think we are," Bags said, or he would have said, if right then an explosion hadn't shaken their world.

"Get down!" It was Gunny yelling, and in the dust and falling debris Bags could make out something had landed in the square.

"What the hell was that?" It was Carmichael yelling now. He'd come up somewhere near Murray and the platoon looked at its forward most men with their eyes wide. Whatever had landed in the square, it had been massive, and the one that followed right then was even worse.

All heads hunkered down.

"Yeah," Bags could hear Gunny now on the radio: "Whatever alternate route we may have had is getting blown to shit. Roger," Gunny continued. "Yep. Roger. I agree." And Bags knew exactly what those rogers now meant. Bags looked at his guys, at Carmichael—who seemed to know, too. "We're moving out!" Gunny then yelled, and not into the radio but down the road. His platoon, his men, all held their rifles and awaited the word: "Let's move!"

They pushed toward the Row. The high walls to Bags's left and right soon squeezed him in, frowning at him as he crept. A round zinged past his head.

Phantom Fury was on. On the platoon's fingertips. On the rooftops as killers shooting down.

The first bullet had been fired at none other than Bags, but as the platoon now surged forward and kept on surging, the second, the third, the seemingly millionth cracked over the head of Hendershot, Carmichael, and every other man as they squeezed against the walls and returned fire.

And because the Marines had trained for shooting upward, they canoed the heads of the figures above them. Because Carmichael was old it took him the longest to hide, and because the IED that had hit Jim's hand hadn't debilitated him, he held his M4 steady and scanned for new targets.

And new targets came. The platoon had decimated the first line of their enemy without losing a man, but now, as new heads popped up from the parapets, a sudden scream ripped through the roadway. It bounced off the walls as if a ball; a bright shriek of agony. One of the Marines had been hit.

Bags, who'd pressed against the right-side wall, was scanning all opposing roofs. The entire right portion of their staggered column was doing so too, as was the left; though their duty was the rooftops above Bags and company's heads. Together, all rooftops were in their rifle sights. They had trained for this exact thing: unbelievable that it was now happening—someone well behind Bags, getting patched up by the corpsman who screamed just as loud it's not fatal and he'd be okay.

Bags steadied his M4, its weight suddenly feeling great. He tried to breathe slow and with some effort he saw the laser-red reticle of his EOTech calm in its shaking. His right hand was around his grip, his index finger straight and off the trigger. A gunfight was so different. Vision pinned. Periphery gone. In the limits of his new sight he saw a silhouette emerging from the protection of the roofs right above Gunny. It was round and black, against the sun, and in a moment it was gone: for Bags had slipped his index finger onto his trigger and gave it a squeeze. Gunny may have thanked him, if he hadn't suddenly had to start squeezing his own trigger.

Gunfire was everywhere. Men were screaming. Radios crackled with useless noise; all interrupted by a strange sound. Despite AK-47s, Bags could still hear it. Yes, that had been glass shattering, but there was something else. And there it was again.

Bags swung his head just in time to see several Marines behind him kick in a door and launch themselves into the building.

LT was on the radio, directing the move. Bags understood in a flash—get up on those roofs! The platoon was terribly vulnerable, no way would they suffer just a single wound. There had to be close to twenty enemy up above, and as the Marines were going inside buildings on both sides, that enemy would soon be met.

It was a strange thing how as the platoon had first entered this urban canyon none had took in the bottom floors. Priorities being what they were, the windows and roofs had demanded their attention. The walls they treaded past had been the mere background of passing cliffs.

But as it were, now Marines infiltrated the first floors, observing their surroundings with new eyes. At LT's behest, team leaders were calling out onto the radios that they were now standing in a used cellphone store, a stairwell leading up to what appeared to be apartments, or, in Bags's case, his team stepped through the already shattered window of a furniture store.

A voice on the radio announced a team had entered a barbershop and had already heard someone scampering back up the stairs. Bags pulled his attention out of his headset and into the room.

Like everything in Iraq, everything in the furniture store looked used. The showroom was small, more a pawnshop where families who'd since fled once browsed couches. The team looked at a set of double doors; open and in the back. Beyond those doors more furniture lay in the gloom; stacked and wrapped in plastic. There was another door, too, in a far corner, open and half-hidden behind a stack of chairs.

From somewhere there came a sound. It was like a broom that had brushed against cardboard. But when it appeared again—"That's a sandal," Jim gasped. "A sandal shufflin'."

A man holding a black-and-brown AK flew into view.

Where he'd come from they had no time to guess, but the burst he laid their way was so loud Bags didn't even hear himself yell "Hit the deck!" Maybe he had. Maybe he hadn't. Maybe gut instinct had put the Marines flat on the floor, then crawling behind cushions before their enemy took off running through the rearward double doors.

Murray was on him. Grass rose and cleared a couch and soon both were lost in the backroom. Gunfire erupted.

"Let's go!" Bags yelled. Jim and Bags were on their feet and running too, but another AK came to life. A man was stepping through that open doorway, aiming over the stack of chairs. The two crunched down and without hesitation they fired, blasting through the chairs and sending the man to the ground.

"They're everywhere!" Jim yelled, and he yelled this more than once, swinging the nose of his M4 from this point to that, sure an ambush was unfolding. Bags listened, and after a time he noticed the gunfight beyond the double doors had stopped.

Jim was closer. He approached the body; Bags right behind him.

The sticky smell of blood hung in the air. Neither had ever seen so much. The floor was plain white tile, but lost was a chunk of it wide and long as a Humvee, now absolutely covered in a bright red pool. In its middle, their man lay crumpled up in a ball, dead, still clutching his heart with both hands. His AK lay strewn across his legs, its barrel pointed slightly upward, no longer smoking.

"You see that, Bags?"

"I do, Jim."

Beyond the dead enemy, beyond his blood, there led

upward a set of stairs. Bags thought of the enemy still up on the roof. And he thought of the members of his platoon still slugging it out with them out on the road.

Jim marched toward the stairs. When he did, he lost his footing, slipping in the enemy's mess, spinning wildly then falling face-first. Covered in blood he cursed and wretched... and then he stopped.

"Bags," he said, almost at a whisper.

Bags had already begun treading carefully toward him, but seeing Jim on all fours and frozen he just stopped. "What? What is it?"

Jim had come eye-level with the dead man's hands. "He's wearing a suicide vest." As Jim scooted away, with some effort Bags could now see that one of the man's hands was around a pull cord.

"Bastard died before he could pull it," Bags said, pulling Jim to his feet. Jim looked at the blood the trail of pinkish white he'd made: the floor reemerging under the blood his scooting had made. Jim looked at what was all over him; especially his forearms and thighs, and he spoke worries over this blood mixing with his own. He was staring at his wounded hand when Bags said, "Where the hell is Murray and Grass?" Jim shrugged. Bags pointed to the stairs, "We clear it first. Then we go find them."

The two walked through the puddle, sidestepping the dead man and his suicide vest. They entered the open doorway and were soon standing at the foot of the stairs. It was a blocky staircase, one that went up a few steps to become a square platform and then twisted to become another flight. Bags was in front and Jim was behind. A two-man clear it was, and they both knew Grass and Murray had to be doing the same. Those other two were close, but even one wall made friends too far when enemies had rifles ready. Those rifles were somewhere up these stairs, so Bags crept slowly; one foot in front of the other, up the sterile white of each. It was at the corners where things became most deadly. Here, grenades could come bouncing down. Here, a turkey-peak could get your jaw shot off. Bags breathed, training his sights upward as he rounded the bend.

"You hear that?" Jim whispered.

"Yes," Bags croaked back. There had been a shuffling of boots. Bags now heard Jim take a step back, then he heard his slow, soft steps to his left. Jim was coming up on his side. They both were going up these stairs; a unified force, four eyes, two rifles, as many bullets as it would take. Bags made the first move.

Shots rang. "Jesus, Mary, and Joseph!" a voice yelled right after. A familiar voice. Bags and Jim ceased their advance, finding Grass standing at the top of the stairs. He'd pulled his SAW high, still holding it toward the ceiling as if an errant round would go off. "I almost took your heads off!—Jim, are you hit? You're covered in—"

"You," Jim growled, so enraged that profanity escaped him. Bags could only turn and gawk at the bullet holes in the wall.

Murray came from around a corner and skidded to a halt. "Bags! Jim! What's everyone…just standing around for?"

"Well," Jim shook, "your *brainy* companion almost splattered *our* brains all over the stairwell." He thumbed back at the evidence and Grass's face ran white. It was an error surely, an egregious one, but Grass soon made up for it as the team shook it off and made for the roof.

"More stairs this way," Grass said, giving Bags and Jim a brief, lively account of how they'd chased their man down and shot him as he was slipping behind an oak buffet. They walked. Murray now led the team, not turning his head when Jim explained what was on him was someone else's, and how it got there. But Grass lit up, saying he'd heard the shots and that he'd heard the very last were M4 and that he'd known that meant they'd come out on top. But more men lurked, they'd heard much foot traffic—what had put him on at the top of the stairwell as Murray had waited for the enemy to come rushing down. Down, as it were, from the metal stairs they now stood in front of, ones leading to the open air of the roof.

They stacked, and they ascended violently, spreading onto the roof like a ring of smoke. One man waited, and Grass took his life.

"Where the hell's the rest of them?" Murray said.

The roof was barren. Shells casing and empty bandoleers lay everywhere. Up out and under the blue sky once more the sounds of Fallujah were ongoing. Mortars impacting were the newest addition, someplace directly to their north.

They fanned out. One Marine per corner, they each walked to their respective edge. Grass insisted he walk toward his kill, being warned loudly by both Bags and Jim that he may have a suicide vest on. Grass yelled back that he didn't...but he had discovered something.

The team rushed over. Grass had already moved it aside with the toe of his boot, but when Bags was at his elbow he kicked it away. A piece of cardboard flew in the air, spray-painted the exact silver-gray of the roof. Under it was a hole.

"An opening," Murray said.

"They sure cut this out in a hurry," Jim said, noting the rough edges. The inner layers of the roof were exposed, like a wild animal had sunk its fangs in and bit in a circle until tearing out a place for the enemy to stare up at them.

Bags jumped back. "If they escaped this way, it means they're still down there." Passing his eyes were visions of AK-47s, pointed up through a crude opening as four heads peered down. "Everyone back up," he said next, his order followed as he then freed a grenade from his chest. He pulled the pin and let it fall, soon being shook by the blast below.

Murray looked him in the eye, "I'm going first." And with that he stood, peeking his head over the rough, serrated edge. "It's a short drop." With that he fell, disappearing into the hole. A moment later they all heard, "all clear!"

It was, in fact, a short distance from the roof to the stack of mattresses Bags had blown to ruin. Smoldering and blackened, they cushioned each Marines' fall, where after the team stood in the living room of a top-floor apartment. Bags went to the window and looked down. They were overlooking the back-side of the building, the side facing away from Insert Bravo.

Jim had already moved to a far corner, guarding a small hallway and whatever waited at its end. Grass and Murray were still moving to their own corners, having first searched under a mattress the grenade had thrown.

There weren't yells of an enemy, and there were not boots or sandals rushing up or down unseen stairs...but there was something. Grass cocked his head like a dog, then his eyes went wide. He pointed to a door against the wall near his corner. It appeared to be a broom closet, and something inside it had fallen. Now every Marine in that living room listened as a muffled squeak was met with a soft, determined "*ssshhh*."

Grass aimed at the door. He was on a knee and an entire SAW drum would obliterate whoever was inside. Bags motioned to him, and he slowly crept over. Bags pressed his back against the wall so that the little door was now directly between he and Grass, and he listened. He listened for what felt like a long while, but he heard nothing more.

Bags seized the small knobby handle and flung the door open.

It seemed instantaneous: the Iraqis that poured out of the closet. Five in all; three children, a woman covered from head to toe, and a man—who then put his hands high as he could, fast as he could, hastily murmuring in broken English that he was "not terrorist."

How they'd all fit in that tiny space no normal man could know, but the team did. They knew the threat of death could make one hide behind a blade of grass. Murray patted the man down. When no weapons were discovered, the Marines watched as he used his hands to help tell a tale.

As best Bags could surmise, the family lived in this apartment and the Muj had barged in weeks ago to cut out their hole. The mattresses had come next. The father believed he and his wife and children were to be human shields. The last gesture the Iraqi made was clear, however many had jumped down that hole and covered it with that gray piece of cardboard, they'd afterward run down Jim's hall.

Gunfire was alive again. It was coming from Insert Bravo. The man gestured if he and his wife could grab some of their belongings and then he pointed toward the hall.

Bags let the family leave. *Human shields*, he thought, not terribly proud of himself, sticking his team behind them; following the Iraqis through a series of doors and down stairs until the Marines were once more boots on the black pavement.

The last he ever saw of that family was them running with their stuff in their arms. There was such fear in the father's eyes, and those children, how dutifully they followed. Bags's thoughts were being pulled back to war, to the hard voice of Gunny Ulfe, but before having done so fully he wondered if that family would make it out of there, and if that father would ever show any face other than fear.

The platoon was regathering. Bags and his team had crawled back out from their building, and when they did he saw more Marines marching or flying out of doors or windows of their own. Across the street, Carmichael had made his way to the forward most edge. He was at Gunny's elbow, shaking his head and agreeing with Gunny about something. Gunny held his M4 tight in his shoulder, and looked ahead at the Row of Four.

The platoon was soon back in its staggered column, sucked tight against the windowed cliffs of their route. Bags could hear with his ears LT, still in the rear; busy on some frequency. Another of their men had been hit: another non-fatal and Bags heard no one screaming. Even the two wounded—three including Jim, who was at Bag's side the way Carmichael was at Gunny's, silent and ready—even the wounded were looking forward. Before them; what Gunny and Carmichael were contemplating, was the bare patch of concrete that separated the north end of Bravo from the first steps of the Row. It was a straight shot, and an enemy sniper's dream. All who'd shot down from the rooftops were now dead; hunted down and slain in stairwells or on the roofs themselves. The Marines pressed against the walls growled about and celebrated their righteous kills: who'd seen what, did what, who'd taken some foe's head off with a three-round burst. New enemy, however, potentially on the roofs of the Four, diminished these celebrations to furtive whispers. Much more was before them, and the battle was still young.

Right then a bongo truck rolled into view. Alarming was its color, for it had been painted from tailgate to grill in a dull black; a black that reflected not the sun but the emptiness of a pointed gun barrel. More alarming still, it had come from behind the building Gunny and Carmichael pressed themselves against, and in what had seemed an instant parked at the platoon's route's northernmost edge. "They're blocking us in," someone behind Bags gasped.

The truck was as long as Insert Bravo was wide, and its passenger side now faced the platoon. Its headlights nearly scraped the wall, and its rear was so close to Gunny that when fighters began spilling out of the driver's side, Bags saw his platoon sergeant rear back as if he'd been kicked. But Gunny was now taking aim. Several barrels pointed at him and he opened fire. There was a return of bullets that came down Bravo like a wall of sheer noise. Somehow Gunny wasn't hit, nor was Carmichael—the old fool—who ducked weaponless as chunks of concrete were ripped from the wall by his head.

Enemy was on the far side of the bongo truck, and Bags and Jim were already shooting. Bags guessed three had slithered out of the driver's door, and he shot at what little of their legs he saw. Jim was obliterating the truck's windshield, yelling something about "their heads!" The entire platoon seemed aimed in on the black bongo. A thunder went up Insert Bravo, ending against the truck's passenger side as it popped and thrummed. But the platoon was shooting at a most determined group. Defiantly, the few behind the truck sprayed and sprayed; pushing the Marines backward. Bags, Jim, Gunny, Carmichael, those nearest to their backs, all fell back as their M4s blared. Before long, Bags saw he was past the very window his team had leaped through to chase the enemy around stairwells and chairs: an enemy far less fierce than those who now blocked their way, and were pushing further.

And then it all happened, and it happened in the time it takes to rack a bullet, shoot it, and watch its casing fall. Gunny was the very first man; the point of the tip of a thrusting spear. He stopped his slow retreat and begin walking forward, the butt of his rifle pressed into the pocket of his shoulder. A fighter charged from behind the truck; leaving the blackened armor to rush down the pavement, spraying wildly. Bags could see Gunny's rounds tearing through the man's chest. This enemy wore a bone-white thobe and blossoms of red continued in their growing. The fighter screamed onward toward them, his AK seemingly unable to run dry.

Gunny came near face to face before putting a bullet through this enemy's brain, and then Gunny Ulfe went to his knees, hot metal in his guts.

There was much chaos. Jim cried out. Bags, not at first believing what his own eyes had told, shot an entire mag into the black truck. Then he got on his radio, crying that Gunny'd been hit, Gunny'd been hit, though LT already knew.

Grass and Murray were behind Bags, a team too clumped together but it mattered not. The four shot at the truck, seeing one foe fall to grab an ankle, and was shot to death for it by more bullets than Bags could count. And all this while, Gunny held his own innards, Carmichael at his side; tearing free a first aid kit. In a moment more, from the corner of Bags's eye he saw LT and Hendershot and two others whose faces were blocked by the down-turned rear of their helmets begin dragging Gunny away. The radio said they didn't stop until inside that barbershop, where LT hopped on a different freq.

Gunny Ulfe would be medevacked, and eventually—though the path was arduous—make near a full recovery and be medically retired. So the bulldog mascot of the Corps, years later, came to make a post that Bags would print and tape to his fridge. Gunny expressed his happiness for having served as long as he had, and how he was grateful for the men whom he forever called friends, brothers, and sons. So, on the whole Gunny fought in Fallujah, and led Marines in missions all over the world. But he never came to the Row of Four.

However, in the meanwhile, the Row of Four loomed a distant, unattainable goal. Gunny was dragged into the barbershop, and Carmichael was there. LT and Hendershot held Gunny Ulfe by his arms, the old man and a Marine from Hendershot's team had him by his legs.

Bags's team was taking it to the enemy. There may have been only one left behind the black bongo, but he'd pulled out a PKM; a long, mean, belt-fed machine gun—and though Bags's guys couldn't see the fullness of their target, there was that firing black barrel, blasting away from over the hood.

But Bags was looking over at the barbershop. Through its cracked windows, he saw the old man trying to console Gunny. Gunny was on the ground and not visible from that angle, but Carmichael was bending down, his arms moving, his mouth speaking slow.

Then the old man's face changed.

From across the street, even with warfare still yanking at his senses, Bags could see how the old man's jaw repositioned. He'd stopped speaking, and as he stood his chin was thrust, the lines of his face seeming to disappear as the sun glared off the glass between them. As the old man stood and peered through the window at the near-distant Row, a glow grew in his eyes. It was soft at first, but it was there, and a moment more Carmichael bent down and Bags lost sight of him.

Then Carmichael was standing once more, this time holding Gunny's M4. Carmichael said something to LT and then walked out of the barbershop, and he slammed the buttstock into the pocket of his shoulder, and, one last time, went to war.

"On me!" Carmichael cried.

"What the...," came from Murray, who'd just rid the earth of the fighter with the PKM.

"On me! On me!" the old man cried, echoing down the street. It was a comical sight—comically sad. An old man had no place here, they'd all known that. But Gunny had allowed it and now Gunny was out, and now the old man was demented enough to yell such insanity? No one would follow him. The Marines looked on, jaws dropped or smirks growing across their faces. They stood as if stricken still, Carmichael marching forward all that while. And the Marines looked on in wonder.

"Your lieutenant," Carmichael cried, "must care for the

fiercest among you! Now you must follow me! To that Row was your errand, and to the Row we must now go! First five: overwatch! All else bound—now!"

"The old man's leading us," Murray gaped, but as he did he saw Grass take a high knee, preparing to take overwatch as the rear members of their marred platoon began rushing forward.

"Thank God," Jim said, joining Grass in open tears.

So it was Murray and Bags who darted across the street, joining Carmichael on his forward march until the three were then kneeling together at their route's furthest edge.

There they looked up at the Row, and the barren space between them and it. Bags heard behind them the rub and jingle of their men's gear. Across the way, Jim was pointing his M4 up at the roofs. Grass was hugging the corner of their wall, knowing the moment the first man passed into that barren space he would need to pop around and provide cover. Bags and Murray were doing the same, and at their side Carmichael kept waving a hand for those coming up behind: *go, go go*!

But right as the first were to break forward, a shot rang out. The unmistakable sound was someone shooting at them from behind; back up on the roofs. Carmichael's waving hand became a fist. "Halt!"

It would remain unknown where exactly the black truck had set out from, but when it first reached the back of the building that Bags, Murray, and Carmichael now knelt against, many enemy had leaped from its bed. Many enemy had entered and the building was alive once more; gunfire from the phone store, a second-floor window, from yet again the perilous rooftops.

LT was yelling on the radio. Caught up in the dust and blood of the rear, still he'd encountered two who'd shouldered through the barbershop's backdoor. The two now lay dead, but his frantic warning of their being swarmed sent Carmichael off his knees.

"This entire thing!" the old man yelled, on his feet, pointing to the building. "It has to be recleared!" The Marines charging forward stopped, following his word without hesitation. And, like that, the rest of the platoon had disappeared. Bags heard the rattle and roar of AKs behind walls, soon met with an answer of M4s.

The rest of the platoon, fighting in the barbershop, throwing grenades behind corners in a used phone store, pointing their short barrels up long stairwells, made it so all who remained on the final stretch of Insert Bravo was Bags and his team. And there was Carmichael. Bags looked now at the Row of Four.

It wasn't just their mission, to hell with missions when blood and guts lay in the street, it was the best vantage point for when their platoonmates emerged back out onto the pavement. High-angle cover was needed, what their platoon needed, what the grunts whom they'd been tasked to serve may desperately need as their awful battle raged on.

Carmichael took the first step. He looked first to his left, then quickly to his right, and the moment he did, Bags and the rest saw him stumble backward, falling onto the concrete sidewalk. It was as if he'd been thrust, being prevented entry toward the Row. A moment more and Bags and Murray both saw enemy creeping around Grass and Jim's corner. Grass and Jim, blocked by their wall, had yet to see. These enemy had sent the old man reeling; who now struggled onto his knees, and he cried, "Contact!"

Grass aimed his SAW now, but as he did a violent *tink* exploded in his face. A terrible jarring went up his hands and he found that his weapon was inert; bore through by a single round. He gasped in fear, stepping backward now himself. The two enemy fighters had come from around the corner that he and Jim guarded, making their way behind the front of the parked truck as they fired. But it had not been a bullet from their AKs that had made Grass's weapon useless. Behind the two fighters, a tall figure also loomed. His face could not be seen, for he wore a dark hood. He was covered from head to toe in black, and he fired from his shoulder a Dragunov rifle.

The three enemy made it behind the black bongo. Then with a rush the two with AKs begin firing down the street. Flames spat out toward the Marines, and behind these rifles the tall man stood leisurely, almost mockingly as he reloaded his weapon.

"Jesus!" cried Grass, who'd dropped to a knee and desperately pulled out pieces of his M4 from his ruck.

Murray gaped as he would at a ghost. "It's that Alzilal!"

"Their leader's back," muttered Carmichael. "Returned with a vengeance." The old man spoke softly, though Bags heard every word. "How I wish I were younger."

The dark figure shouldered his rifle and took aim. The two men in his foul charge yelled and missed every Marine they shot at. Then Murray zeroed in on one of their mouths and let a bullet fly. For a moment the fighter stood there, as if stunned, then the man fell back, and the dark figure behind him aimed his sights again.

"To the Row!" cried Carmichael, rising. "Get to the Row of Four! Rush forward and let us slip beyond this barricade. Move!" Bags and Murray did not move, but shot at that barricade until the two behind it had no choice but to duck for cover. Grass had not yet assembled his rifle, and in this agonizing span Jim could only serve as his guardian; joining the others in their blast toward the truck.

The leader of the Alzilal whistled. Carmichael was aiming, wobbling to his feet, waiting, but the two enemy were now unseen. The old man held Gunny Ulfe's M4, mumbling something about "this infernal television screen." *It must be the EOTech he's referring to*, Bags thought. Then the leader of the Alzilal whistled louder.

"I'm up!" Grass yelled from across the way. And as his words were still being spoken, more enemy rounded the corner —this time nearest Bags. This force was far more than two, and the lead man almost came nose-to-nose with Carmichael. But then the old man fired, and when he began firing he did not stop. The rest of the platoon was rattling the very walls of the buildings behind him, with M4s, with SAWs that still worked, but in this new and sudden chaos it seemed to Bags that the only weapon that mattered was the old man's. Enemy dropped in heaps, and when it was time to change magazines Carmichael did so with great struggle. M4s were foreign, and so Bags and Murray, recalling their plight, shot down all others who poured around that corner until their leader was "guns-up!" once more.

"To the Row!" cried Bags and he leaped forward.

At that moment Carmichael shouldered his weapon, and yelling he fired at the truck as he moved. The weapon was aimed well. Blood sprayed from the chest of the dark figure. Two things had happened; the last of the Alzilal had risen, and Carmichael had timed that final rise.

With a terrible moan the Alzilal fell forward, and blood ran to the earth. But even as he fell he swung up his rifle, and the Dragunov lacerated the air.

There was no way to know how many men Carmichael had killed—his weapon accidently put on safe, a curse then flicked back to fire, and then it all had begun again: faces taking bullets and Muj falling back and collapsing into the street where they laid lifeless and bleeding. And in the end that Dragunov bullet had found him. He'd survived Korea, Vietnam, and God only knew, to fall in Fallujah, shot dead with one round through the heart.

The rifles now stopped firing, and silence fell. The team stood aghast in horror, staring at Carmichael. Even as Grass and Jim came running over, they were already in tears. With a wince, Bags slapped in a fresh magazine.

"Move!" he commanded. "Let's move—we'll come back. Follow me."

The team walked intently toward the Row. The barren space was before them. On this they moved. Bags heard Jim crying, and then he found that he was crying too. Gunfire had reentered, and noises of their platoon emerging back onto the pavement of Insert Bravo filled their ears.

Right then a clear shot rang out, and all heard it but Bags for he'd taken it directly in the armor plate covering his chest. More shots followed, but for Bags's instant slump to the ground he may have been killed. The last fighter who'd sunk behind the bongo truck was still there, and his AK ran out of bullets as Murray, Jim, and Grass gunned him down. Grass said later that he at first wanted to take that fighter's AK, for he'd grown so used to his SAW that an M4 felt light and strange.

In the end it was not Bags, but Jim; Jim who helped drag Bags into the Row of Four, Jim who climbed to a roof and gave coordinates to Murray who relayed them to LT who had arty rain down hellfire on the city until many enemy were vanquished and the platoon was safe. Bags had taken a blast so fierce that for a time he could not breathe, and he worried in his wartorn mania that he'd never breathe again. Somewhere in a room within the Row he found he was stripped bare and work began on tension pneumothorax. He was to be stuck by an evil great needle, but those in attendance rejoiced, greatest of which was Bags himself, for it was determined that he'd merely lost his wind, and owned one severely bruised rib. The bullet that had knocked him flat had also found a way to break his skin, and as artillery shells landed and the sun began to set, a voice that he could not identify reminded him he'd be put in for another Purple Heart.

The next morning they were on a roof. The whole team was there. The Row's rooftops were so close together that they could leap from one to the next. Bags, pressing the palm of his hand against his rib and still wincing, left such feats to Murray or Grass. Neither jumped nor moved joyously, though. Nor did the rest of the platoon. LT was on the radio, talking endlessly to someone who hadn't seen what they had.

No more planes were dropping bombs. No more howitzers were blasting shells out over miles of earth. No more mortars were falling. No more PKMs, or PRGs, or AK-47s, or dreaded Dragunov rifles. The early morning had risen over the city's edge; its blasted and barren rooftops where Fallujah met the farmlands, and in that golden haze Grass began fishing through his rucksack.

Bags watched as Grass knelt. With a grunt, Grass pushed aside his broken SAW. He had shoved it in his ruck nose-down, as if to forget about it, and from somewhere underneath its muzzle he pulled out a long-contemplated prize. And it made Bags smile.

The Listerine bottle was one of those travel-size kinds, and it was full of good, hard whiskey.

The platoon was guarding the roof, and those facing east all watched as droves of armored vehicles entered the city. "The cleanup crew," someone said. Bags couldn't help but then imagine a possible horror—as more soldiers and Brits overwhelmed Fallujah to pick off stragglers, what if a few enemy would slip out of the net and bunker down back in the farmlands? Surely knock-and-talk efforts would recommence. No greater threat existed than weary warriors who've let down their guard. And after this monumental push, how could they not? Something close to that had made them forget an armed man who was a mere twenty feet from them, behind a bongo truck they'd put a hundred rounds through. And that man had nearly cost Bags his life. He tried to breathe in a little deeper, stopped short by the shock of pain.

"Farewell, old man," Grass said, saluting the sidewalk below them and he knocked back a swig. Bags nodded when Grass handed him the bottle and he took his pull.

"LT said Gunny the body are on the same plane home,"

Bags said, the finest-tasting thing in all his life running down his throat. Jim and Murray joined them and each in turn drank their share until the bottle was gone. A "nation-builder" perhaps would have stowed his trash, but Grass let the bottle fall.

Now as the platoon sat or walked amongst the four roofs they spoke of Carmichael, and all that each had known of him and learned from him. As their energy replenished and wounds ached and began already to heal, the weight of their loss grieved them all the greater. Often they thought of Gunny, and what pain he must be enduring; how he would have done anything to see his men through their most difficult errand. How they'd done it without him, though without his mentorship all doubted that they would have been so able. And such mentorship had shined in a new light with the sudden leading by Carmichael, the return of a warrior whose final hour put even the hardest member of the platoon on their knee, or off in quiet somewhere to shed tears alone.

It was Bags who saw the last explosion. Some mortar team with a round to kill, or some enemy clinging on just long enough to show death was welcome and pulled his cord. A brief blast down an alley, followed by the smoke and rubble and then a silence so pure it was as if the world had found a mute button. What broke it was Marines laughing. Grass slapped Bags on the shoulder and disappeared to cavort with members of other teams. They had marched to the city to retake it, and they had infiltrated its streets and in their doing men were injured and a man died. The sun rose and with it the autumn heat. Bags felt for a moment that he would fall; off the roof, off the world. But Jim was there to steady his wobble and together they laughed. The retaking was over.

One month to the day later, the platoon was back in the farm-lands. Operation Phantom Fury still lingered, and would until officially ending on the 23rd of December. But this day was December 8, and though the occasional howitzer spat its pow-er, LT let his men play shirtless football.

The day was green and the Iraq sun burned with less a sneer as it does in the summer, and the platoon's work within the city was long since done. Pushing in like a knife's blade to become the eyes and ears for commanders had resulted in many missions. The men on those roofs had called in artillery and fixed wing, and from behind the glass of M40 sniper rifles those trained to do so delivered lethal long-range precision fire. After three days atop the Row of Four, the platoon—whole, save for a few wounds—departed Fallujah under the watchful eye of LAV-25s.

Four of them in total: rhino-like, eight-wheeled armored vehicles escorting them down Insert Bravo and back again onto bare earth. Technically built for amphibious work, much like the Recon Marines themselves the LAVs were in this way far out of place; and at least one dark poet among the men stated the only fluid to wade through was that of blood. Though, that by then was drying.

Now in the tilled fields of the Zaidon, the lands south of the city suffered a small blemish as a burly warrior caught a Hail Mary and crashed into the dirt. He rose to much applause and threw the football back to LT; who'd promoted himself to quarterback. More violence would come to the land, one of which being Bags's final brush with death, but for now they'd killed or locked up who'd needed to be, and perhaps that meant a job well done.

The few who didn't play stood guard in the trucks. Mounted behind machine guns and grenade launchers they watched more of the game and less of their fields of fire. Though they wore their body armor they kept it loose around the chest. No helmet was on a single head as the men soaked up the sun as music from someone's boom box played. *Nirvana*, *CKY*, and of course *Creedence*: CDs switched out by Bags; who'd become DJ after having suffered a bad tackle that had aggravated his rib.

Jim and he and all others who were wounded except for Gunny had received their Purple Hearts in an emotional formation back in Camp Fallujah. They stood after what could only be deemed a victory: a victory because those who'd taken aim at their lives had died and they had lived. It was a hard truth that two members of a brother platoon had met a bitter end down a long hallway elsewhere in the city, and to them the chief honor of the formation went. Yet, despite the somber reminder of this loss, those in attendance felt exuberance. They had joined to go to war, and in so doing had gone. They were older now, not grown wiser by the passage of time but by the sheer lightning pace of the miles that had flown underneath their boots. Boots that had been caked in mud and blood and the vile remnants of a city before it had been converted into a trap for death.

Bags was slowly putting on his gear. His undershirt went on, then his cammie blouse next. It first had that laundry smell of Camp Fallujah; over-cleaned, almost a bleach odor. It had been stiff and starchy but now a few days sweat outside the wire had it back to right. Bags shrugged his flak jacket on and tightened it to his chest. He laughed as Murray leg tackled poor Hendershot.

"Sir," the comm guy said from LT's Humvee, wiggling a handset out the window. "Telephone."

Bags sucked from a water bottle as he watched LT toss the ball and jog over. Radio traffic had been slow as of late; mostly mandatory comm windows where all there was for the platoon to report was the number of knock-and-talks they'd conducted. No weapons had been found. No more zip ties had been used. The Iraqis who'd made their way back to their homes greeted the Americans with the plastic and wary courtesy that most would when armed men stood in the front yard.

Easy days had led to throwing the old pigskin, but now Bags saw LT was snapping his fingers to the comm guy; signaling for a pen. The lieutenant then began writing down notes and saying "Roger that, sir" and soon was calling for the platoon to gather round.

"Hey, listen up," LT said. "About four klicks south, there's farmhouses we're going to go clear. Intel came in at least one is being used as an armory. As we all know, the Muj isn't done. Anything we find, we'll detonate on sight." Shirts came back on, and gear was again over their shoulders and chin straps tightening as the lieutenant continued. Their mission was to clear the farmhouses and haul out and blow any enemy ordnance, but also to confirm or deny the rumor that a remnant of anti-coalition forces were regathering. A large net had to have a few holes.

Along the way, LT let the boom box play. It was some techno mix that everyone hated save for the comm guy, and as the platoon rolled down the hardball the sequenced beats echoed off the walls of street-side barbershops and unshot-at mosques.

The farmhouses were three in number, placed along the end of a dirt path that lead off from the road. The houses were surrounded by fields. The platoon staged their vehicles as they had the whole deployment; in the shape of an L, leaving a turret gunner as every other team member set out on foot.

Grass had been deemed the stay-behind, and as he sat up in the turret Bags told Jim and Murray that LT had said they were to clear the middle house. By the lack of bongo trucks, it seemed no one was home. Prior to Fallujah, these types of missions were often met with men standing outside, waving. They were docile waves, never friendly, but it clued the Marines in that locals were on sight.

Two teams had ganged up on the near house, and the final team was still marching toward the third as Bags raised his fist to knock on the door.

"What am I doing?" he said, shaking his head. "Guys, let's stack. Sorry." Jim and Murray were already pressed against the wall when he took the tail-end, squeezing Jim and initiating the chain.

Bags heard the doorknob creak as Murray turned it and a moment more they stood in three corners of the standard Iraqi living room. No one was home, and below their feet was a carpet so clean Bags instinctively lifted his boot to ensure its tread wasn't caked with some mess. There were colored pillows in the corners and a low table where the missing family had sat and drank chai. Jim was looking at a hallway leading off into shadows. Murray moved toward an open wall and said there was a kitchen.

"Go ahead and check it, Murray," Bags said, moving toward Jim. "Jim and I will clear the hall." As Bags moved he was stopped by an amusing sight. One of the living room walls seemed to protrude a bit, like the builder hadn't gotten in quite right and had later packed on more stucco to set things correct. On the middle of this wall, there hung a large portrait.

"You think this place belongs to a sheik?" asked Jim.

Bags could hear Murray in the kitchen, rummaging and opening cabinet doors. "Maybe," Bags said, and he looked at the subject in the portrait, understanding why Jim asked. He was a tall man, definitely Iraqi, ordained in a shemagh set with golden stitch. His thobe was made of black and white and in front of it he clasped his hands; one of them, around it, a bright gold watch. What had made Bags stop was not this man's fine position. What made Bags laugh was the man stood next to a rolled-out canvas; its wheels still visible, and on this prop was a half-good painting of the Golden Gate Bridge. Be in Iraq but pose like you're in America. All the Americans here were eating up disposable cameras to take their photos while standing in front of blue-domed mosques or cars burned beyond recognition.

Bags was behind Jim and they flowed like a cool stream down the hall. A few thresholds without doors: a few empty rooms: a few "clears." Any rug they came across they lifted by a corner and checked for trap doors. Though their platoon had never come across one, grunts in the city had reported they'd stumbled on dozens.

"I bet there's stuff in the berms," Jim said, looking out the back window now. Bags and Jim were in the farthest room down the hall and Bags heard Murray's boots soon coming their way. A moment more they all stood together, reporting there was nothing in the house and agreeing that LT needed to see if they could get some engineers for the berms.

"One metal detector," Murray said with a yawn, "then call it a day."

Bags laughed, "Sounds like the day's just beginning." His head was cocked and Murray and Jim could see he was listening to his headset. Murray hadn't even packed the big radio. Everyone was so close a good shout did the job. Bags, by sheer habit, had donned his MBITR and now he relayed to Jim and Murray that, "The guys in the first house found a cache." Bags repeated their discoveries as their platoonmate on the radio listed them for LT. "Five AKs," he said. "Two RPGs—old ones —two PKMS and bags of ammo."

There was more. Stuffed inside a stack of tires, the weapons and ammo were pulled out, and along with them came blasting caps by the hundreds. Next to the tires sat, unbelievably, a 55-gallon drum of TNT.

"LT sounds excited," Bags said. "He's calling EOD."

The three watched from Jim's window as a brother team marched out into the fields. Good fortune had their discovery be made in the house where two teams had been searching. It was Hendershot who now jogged into view, his rifle slung behind him, carrying a shovel. The three laughed as he began to dig; probably cursing his rotten luck. Soon the cache was in a fresh hole; deep enough to swallow machine guns and far enough from the houses that the drum being rolled toward it wouldn't level the entire neighborhood. The Marines worked like ants until the blow sight was ready. All they needed next was the arrival of EOD.

Bags and his guys began making their way back to the Humvee. Bags walked slowly, still listening to the chatter on the radio. As he made his way into the living room, something pulled him from his headset. It sounded like a crack, or a scrape. It could not have come from Murray or Jim; they were already out the front door. The noise had come from behind him. Bags turned to see a man coming out of the wall.

The wall was opening! The wall with the portrait of the well-groomed Iraqi standing by a fake Golden Gate Bridge. It had been a false wall—a tactic that would be used more and more as the war effort raged—and from this stucco, still emerging, was a military-aged male. *This* man was not dressed in fine cloth. *This man* was not clasping his hands. Faster than a single heartbeat, Bags saw his gray thobe, his ragged beard, his terrified, hateful eyes; white and widened. He was holding an AK-47, and it was pointing straight at him.

Bags couldn't know if the man had been insane, or if he'd thought the coast was clear, if he'd looked through the tiniest of cracks and felt the time was finally right, or if he'd just grown sick of hiding. The enemy stepped out and Bags and he blasted at each other. The enemy was killed. Bags was left sprawled out on the floor, holding a hole in his arm.

Much happened. EOD finally did arrive. An explosion like no other sent dirt and flame and a hellish roar, leaving a massive crater. But first, another AK was added to the pile, and Bags was rushed out of the farmlands and placed in a gown in Camp Fallujah.

Squirming in pain and then floating in morphine, Bags knew the hospital bed he was lying in was not going to give him back. His war, his part, was over. Two days later he began a bumpy ride back to the States.

Economists and philosophers will say that all societies operate on a seesaw. Seated on one end is Equity; the maidenhead of a postmodern age. Seated at the other is Efficiency; the hardened mother of the Model T, the Orville brothers' first plane, and the mother of what burned lustfully in their inventors. The balance is never perfect. One side always wins. One rider weighs more: pulls harder toward the earth. "And that's not all!" will say the economists and the philosophers and now the historians, who will rightly declare that attached to the pursuit of excellence can come something like dignity…though not felt by all, for not all may grow wings. And they will say that with our steady march now toward whatever awaits us at the other end, we march there by way of our envy, and by recounting transgressions against us with a darkened glee.

Corporal Tyler Boggs—Bags, who flew out of Iraq to Germany—passed over the eastern coast of this land, his land, on his way from Maine to North Carolina. And as he passed he did not yet know the full extent of its decline, though early signs were there.

One was being a veteran. A wounded one, at that. The PTSD contagion caught on fast, and when it did it did not relent until every news station and advocacy group had their fangs in the throat of every piece of meat who'd donned a uniform. It was the GWOT who was the very first: perhaps unknowingly becoming the poster children, to tout the new banner, to gobble down hook, line, and sinker the crowd-roar of Victim. Even with three Purple Hearts and a nicked humerus, what nightmares he had he'd quickly gotten over. The worst feeling was not being out there with his friends, or to return with them; as one.

When a unit returned they "retrograded." Bags sat on that word, *retrograde*—to go backward—in his barracks alone, scratching his bandaged arm. His parents had hugged him the moment he'd stepped foot off the bus and back onto the cool wintered soil of Camp Lejeune. They'd afterward gone out to eat and he'd told them much of what happened and no one talked about his sister. He said he would be going on leave in a few days and he'd see them again soon. Then he was alone, in his room, annoyed at an arm that was slowly healing. And he thought about that word "retrograde" and how those who'd put the buttstock of a weapon into the pocket of their shoulder, greased by the brutal sun, trekking a foreign land and witnessing rot and the dead, death and entropy, and how, no matter how much they may have missed their home, their truck, their parents, when the time came to fly back they were all indeed, yes, in retrograde.

Some weeks after returning to Camp Lejeune, Bags was in his mother's home. There, he had been greeted with a hero's welcome. Aunts had hugged him and step-uncles had asked to see his arm. It was no longer in a sling, but bandaged; a simple white cloth he could slip aside and poke the nickel-size wound that would purple as the years passed. He had gone to the river with his dad and from the dock Bags and he talked about much; about his dad's dead brother, hope for his sister, they spoke together about the beauty of the wetlands and Bags knew that he and his father now shared something no differences could break. They'd served. Their wars, so different, allowed them to watch the bobbers float calmly and not another word be muttered.

Bags boarded a plane soon after. The battalion was still deployed and he flew across the country to stand at Karl Carmichael's funeral in his dress blues, drunk.

A private family funeral had been held already, but Bags

had been told by the skeleton crew manning Battalion head-quarters back in Lejeune that the old reporter was to be given a formal send-off. It had been put together by the VFW and the magazine Carmichael had worked for.

In a large chapel hugging the coast, Bags met Carmichael's family; a little platoon all its own; filled with daughters and grandchildren, some not far off in age from Bags himself. Carmichael had his own younger sister. She had, *of course*, Bags laughed to himself, served in the Corps too, and appeared to be the host of the ceremony. She asked Bags to take the front row; where he stood and thought about Carmichael's grandkids, wondering if he'd wanted them to tie their boots and go off to war, or if he'd hoped they'd just stay home. Bags had drank much that day, starting on the plane ride the night before and continuing at his hotel. Bags wobbled, hiding his breath as best he could.

The ceremony began, and when it did Bags felt the tears run down his cheeks. The preacher spoke and Bags listened, soon no longer hearing the words. More than words and sniffs and grateful sobs had filled the chapel. A great man had died, and he'd died on his terms. He'd served and he'd led his family, as he'd served and led so many men, some of whom stood behind Bags in uniforms of their own.

When it was over, Bags turned and gazed upon them, dress blues and alphas—a sea of dark blue, red and green. And they approached him, some of them his father's age, some of them old and gray, bent by time, erected by the uniform for a short while more. They all eyed the purple hanging from Bags's chest and they shook his hand. They told stories of Carmichael in Vietnam, as a rigid platoon sergeant in the garrison days and they asked Bags to tell the story of what had put them all there. And Bags did, somewhere in it feeling much the fool when he recounted how the old man had said if he "bought the ranch" Bags could have his motorcycle.

Bags hadn't realized the size of the crowd that had gathered. Many attendees stood behind him, most of them Carmichael's family. All had listened but it was Carmichael's sister who appeared then at Bags's side, having shouldered through. And she did not weep. She smiled. In her hands—old Marines laughed and Bags was in disbelief—dangled a set of keys. She then pulled from her purse a rolled-up folder full of notes. "These were his," she said. "His magazine likes them, but he wrote so much about you that we want you to finish it." Leaving Bags stunned she told him an address and somewhere after in that surreal blur the funeral was over.

Hours later, still in his uniform and still drunk, Bags had the machine beneath him—a Harley Davidson Sportster, 883ccs; not much for a Marine in his twenties but some serious muscle for a man who'd almost touched seventy-three. Bags had never rode a bike before, not on his own. But he'd jumped out of planes and helicopters and knew the awesome power of momentum. He'd take things slow, learn the gears. He made sure the headlight was on and laughed there would be no Kevlar for this.

It was night, and like a Recon Marine embarking on his patrol, cocking up the kickstand with his dress shoe he rolled onto the hardball. The folder and a battle's worth of notes were in a saddlebag, and he breathed in deep. He started in a neighborhood, thinking only of shifting and balance and how touchy the brakes were…but in a matter of minutes he thought of no such things, having sped out onto a main road and now the sound of the engine was in his ear, the thrum of the chassis under his weight and before him a vacant open road that stretched to someplace that he did not know…and he did not care.

There was no armor this night, nor were there rules, and no breaking at the curves once he got a feel for his new machine. Well, one rule: the stop sign he nearly blew past but broadsided to a halt before the thick white line across the road. He had no clue where he was, only that he'd flown into some business strip and he needed to find a highway. A sign that pointed him toward exactly that stood under a streetlight.

He was in first gear, spitting a bug out and pulling back on the throttle—thirty, forty—then he worked the clutch clumsily and broke into second, rolling up an on-ramp, looking out as he entered the main lanes for another free man who might be flying past. He was alone…and with a wide open roadway he pulled back again…then third gear came, pushing seventy and the wind began to scream. He had to squint, for the blasts on his eyeballs could feel like a sandstorm.

He bent forward, sparing his eyes from the wind as he and his bike passed under a tall light. Bags held his grip on the handlebars and in that moment he saw it, and once he did he looked at it more, almost wrecking, his gas tank paint job of an eagle caught in flight, its beak open; an eternal scream of glory as the bike soared past an abandoned car.

More abandoned cars were here, ones that looked torched by flames or had orange square stickers on their windows with looming threats of being towed…it's the rut in the route with all the trash on the road, the aftermath of the retrograde, and

Bags negotiated the debris without losing control, without crashing, without becoming the headline: "Iraq War Vet Crashes Due to PTSD."

Having negotiated the trash, the gear went up to fourth, and now his eyes and ears were numb. Fifth gear came and Bags felt his bullet wound burning, the muscles in that arm unfamiliar with these new demands. His medals flew off, leaving only his Purple Hearts as his burning eyes strained to make out when the next curve would appear.

But with such speed, with the needle having crept close to one hundred and still creeping, with no eye protection and whiskey surging through his veins, curves and cars, debris, and maybe a lurking cop, they all would appear after it's already too late. And that was when Bags throttled back until it could be pulled no further. He could barely see. Tears from a funeral, from being back when his men still needed him, tears of fantastic joy that come at a hundred miles an hour; all blown back with the exhaust. He could not feel his arm anymore, nor his hands, only the hard metal howl rumbling between his legs. He stayed close to the center lines...leaning through a curve to the right, then right again and he blew past a huge green sign he thought said "exit"...and he let off, regaining his vision, but only just enough to see another dark stretch that needed flying down. To fly: who can say why so many feel its need? But the feeling is there, in young men wishing for their own noble war, for those who stretch their luck so far that fear becomes a drug; plunging deeper than any needle. Bags pulled back, and slowed down, and he took the next off-ramp.

In the parking lot of a fast food joint, he sat on the Sportster as its engine cooled. Quiet now, someplace close to midnight, his arms and hands and whole body tingled. His eyes were dry and his ears were still ringing, and enough liquor had run its course so that he could contemplate his lunacy. He was looking out over the coast, westward, and he felt he could go on forever.

Throughout the long flight home Bags opened up his back-pack and looked at his souvenir. It was not the pamphlet from Carmichael's funeral, nor the notes he'd been given, nor was it the receipt the moving company had handed him when he'd given up the Sportster and paid for it to be driven through the fly-over states to reunite at the door of his dad's garage. He held a leaflet; one he'd taken off the roof in Iraq out from that pallet that had failed to disperse.

He looked at the depiction of Iraqis running for their lives and somewhere over the Midwest he imagined a new leaflet, one to be dropped by the millions: Americans, running out of American cities. But they are not fearful, they are smiling, a trail of filth in their wake, as it appears they are about to run up a hill and continue up into the air.

To soar free, one must not only harden one's self for war but go and fight it. Whatever *it* may be. In the streets, in the desert of another's country, or in the impoverished desolation of one's own soul. Liberation demands blood and sweat and… this is the only way, at least for us.

Now Tyler Boggs thinks about death and he thinks back to the skeleton they saw on the march to Fallujah. He can't remember if anyone ever went back to gather the bones, scoop them up, or see who they used to be. But he remembers now something his eyes had seen but his heart and brain had been too laden to understand. That sun-bleached skull: out of an eye socket had been growing a desert flower.

Death brings life, and ends bring beginnings.

He grabs the stack of pages with both hands and packs them against the wood of his desk until they are once more a solid block. He mouths the title he gave it, "In and Out of Fallujah," finally satisfied that it'll do.

He stands and he puts away the crinkled leaflet, the Purple Hearts he owns without pride or shame. And he puts away the gas caps, and as he does they remind him of life; how lucky he was, how lucky all are to be alive, here this short while. Caught in this great cycle, like the turn of a great bike's wheel.

Then he shuts the closet door and turns and looks at all the pictures on the wall: Murray with his wife and their dogs, Pendergrass with his wife and their brand-new son, and of course Sergeant Major Theodore James; still in, and with more ribbons on his chest than God, grinning, one kid per deployment, with that gleam in his eye.

The sun was setting and through his blinds the window shined through yellow and orange. There was a knock at the door and Tyler's wife came in. Her motorcycle helmet was already on. "Sitter's here," she said. "We going?"

He turned off the lights. "We are," he said.

DEAD RECKONING
2017
COLLECTIVE

DEAD RECKONING COLLECTIVE is a veteran owned and operated publishing company. Our mission encourages literacy as a component of a positive lifestyle. Although DRC only publishes the written work of military veterans, the intention of closing the divide between civilians and veterans is held in the highest regard. By sharing these stories it is our hope that we can help to clarify how veterans should be viewed by the public and how veterans should view themselves.

Visit us at:

deadreckoningco.com

@deadreckoningcollective

@deadreckoningco

@DRCpublishing